Just like the Sky River Rock Festival event, the historical fiction of Before Woodstock — The Sky River Rock Festival & Lighter Than Air Fair was over too soon. A fascinating tale with a love story, coming-of-age adventure, and plenty of factual information about the festival. J.D. deeply researched the history of a unique event and captures the vibe of that era perfectly. One can almost hear the music and smell the patchouli. Well-paced and complete, Before Woodstock covers the background of events leading up to those three magical days. Highly recommended, this publication is a gift, helping us to remember those long past events.

Steve Noe ~ Sky River attendee and son of general manager Cyrus Noe

A reticent journalist's assignment to cover a rock festival becomes a transformative experience in JD Howard's historically accurate novel that recreates, not only the sights and sounds of one of America's first rock festivals, but the first flowering of a cultural revolution that changed the world.

Bill White ~ former arts reviewer for the Seattle P-I

JD's story is just plain fun! Well researched and lovingly put together. Bravo!

Gale Fiege ~ retired Everett Herald reporter, who was 11 years old when she attended the festival with her dad, Gene Fiege. A Mountlake Terrace city councilman, WWII veteran and supporter of the Helix and KRAB radio, Gene said, "Let's go see what those hippies are up to."

Before Woodstock

The Sky River Rock Festival & Lighter Than Air Fair

J. D. Howard

Cover & chapter art work: Steve Breeden

Back cover photo: Tore Ofteness

Author at: beforewoodstock1968@gmail.com

Son Earth Publishing

Library of Congress Catalog in Publication Data
has been applied for

ISBN: 978-1-7336043-5-2

To all our Rock-n-Roll Heroes of the '60s

Pleased To Meet You
(Introduction)

In 1968 the United States was awash in conflict both at home and abroad. Known by some as the year of law and disorder, it was a flashpoint in time that was a turning point in America. From the politics to the battlefield, to even the music, it was a year that our nation was rocked to its core. The federal government, which had long been viewed as the protector of our sacred Constitution and promoter of truth and justice for all, was now seen by the Youth Movement as an imposter who no longer filled that role and had lied to them.

President Lyndon Johnson's grand 'nation building' vision of ending Communism and bringing Democracy to Vietnam had manifested into a bloody quagmire when he escalated the conflict in January with the

Battle of Khe Sanh. Soon thereafter the Tet Offensive began and with it a growing media coverage that caused dramatic shifts in how the war was perceived in the American public and particularly the young, who began to question if we were still the good guys.

When Muhammad Ali refused to be drafted because of his religious beliefs, he spoke out against the war. The younger generation listened. After he was convicted of draft evasion and his boxing titles stripped away, Ali became a signpost and inspiration to those who believed that the war in Vietnam was wrong. He helped give the young adults of America the courage to stand up and protest against a senseless conflict.

Anti-Vietnam protesters filled the streets in every major city chanting 'Hell no, we won't go' and the near nightly television reports of body counts greatly contributed to the country's growing distaste of the fighting, clearly showing that we were losing. Disgruntlement was in the air and in the minds of everyone who was paying attention.

The nation was still reeling from the King and Kennedy assassinations when the Democratic National Convention in Chicago erupted in violence both inside and out of the convention hall. Police brutality was captured live by television cameras.

The political climate was reaching a boiling point, and daily turmoil caused many to take to the streets demanding change, not only in our politics but in our culture as well. Topic driven music with brave lyrics blared from nearly every hip radio station and most stereo systems. Music was the best and loudest voice the youth had not only for guidance but for real transformation. In a nation damaged and torn apart by the war, music was the one thing that brought young people together, it was the common denominator. It lifted spirits, provided an escape, and gave the youth permission to forget about all of the troubles that surrounded them.

The beginnings of the Youth Movement and New Left can be traced back to 1962 when the Students for a Democratic Society (SDS) drafted the *Port Huron Statement.* It emphasized the importance of individual action and responsibility, a society that prioritized social justice and equality, and criticized America's Cold-War foreign policy among many other noted points.

In *The Last Great Dream,* author Dennis McNally points to poets Kenneth Rexroth and Robert Duncan who, without knowing it, lit the torch of literary art that became the Beat Movement. But when Lawrence Ferlinghetti published Allen Ginsberg's poem *Howl,* it became one of the most important poems in American history and shined a spotlight on the many creative people of San Francisco. That and the San Francisco Art Institute, where a student learned 'art isn't what you do, but who you are' and where artistry replaced conventional expressions of religion. The SFAI helped the many talented people there move realism into surrealism through the rejection of violence and placed freedom before authority, and creativity ahead of consumption.

The Beat Generation's literary subculture movement of the 50s, fueled by the rejection of materialism through poetry, spontaneous prose, and jazz, had transcended into the *Summer of Love* the year before. The Beat's ideology manifested into and was fully embraced by the Hippie Movement and gave way to a whole new world of free-thinking, free love, and a youth culture that told their parents they were now rejecting their value systems and going to be heard, which in turn caused massive revision.

In 1968 television brought us *The Mod Squad* that tested the viewing public by combining a black man, a fairy like flower child blonde woman, and a longhaired white guy, who'd been rejected by his wealthy parents, with its themes of the fast-changing times. Using slang terms like 'solid' and 'keep the faith' the show was one of the first to have a black man kiss a white woman on the TV screen. *Hawaii Five-0* made the long arm of the law appear popular to some by opening with a rock music theme and hip-shaking smiling hula girl that grabbed the attention of every teenager right down to the catchphrase 'Book 'em Danno.' America's favorite Beatnik, Maynard G. Krebs of *Dobie Gillis* fame, could still be found on afternoon reruns. In it, Krebs was stereotypically portrayed as a bongo playing, lazy, slang speaking bohemian best remembered for his distaste of Lawrence Welk and his cringing allergic reaction at the mere utterance of the word 'work' in his presence.

Bullitt starring Steve McQueen and Jacqueline Bisset was one of the first movies to be filmed almost entirely on location but Stanley

Kubrick's science fiction film, *2001: A Space Odyssey* was the highest grossing film that year earning $56 million. Its supercomputer HAL caused most to question the possibility of a manmade machine that could take over the world. *The Odd Couple* starring Walter Matthau and Jack Lemmon as two incompatible bachelors sharing a Manhattan apartment made America laugh in spite of the turmoil that was disrupting the country at the same time that *Night of the Living Dead* terrified audiences with its zombie horror scenes.

In the art world Peter Max became a counter-culture icon who created colorful commercial art that graced posters and covers of publications with what he called his *Cosmic '60s Period.* Andy Warhol was another leading figure of pop art who dabbled in silkscreen, painting, and both erotic and experimental movies. Warhol survived an assassination attempt on his life by Valerie Solanas, a 32-year-old feminist who was angry at Warhol over debts she believed he owed her from her theater script *Up Your Ass* and her novels manuscript. Inside Warhol's Factory studio in Manhattan, Solanas fired three shots at him, hitting Warhol once in the stomach. In the emergency room he was declared dead but the surgeon massaged his heart and revived him. Solanas was arrested and eventually served time for first degree assault.

The mini-skirt and the *Mod Swinging London Styles* of Mary Quant and Carnaby Street were left behind and replaced with batik and tie-dye T-shirts, headbands, beads, bracelets, and the shabby chic clothes found at the local Goodwill. Street styles replaced high fashion which was left on the closet floor right next to khaki slacks while Levi 501 jean sales climbed sharply.

On vinyl poet laureate Bob Dylan had disappeared since his motorcycle accident until *The Mighty Quinn* single dropped by Manfred Mann. Dylan moved back into his self-realized Americana style of acoustic driven songs on *John Westley Harding* which included *All Along the Watchtower* that Jimi Hendrix reinterpreted so masterfully that same year.

The Rolling Stones created the mythical imagery of *Jumpin' Jack Flash* who moved into *Street Fighting Man* and then took flight through the current struggles of life and death in *Symphony for the Devil* on *Beggar's Banquet* turning the rock world on end with its vivid lyrics. The Beatles seminal *White Album* put conservative households on their collective ear with McCartney's *Why Don't We Do It in the Road* and *Back in the U.S.S.R.* while Lennon's *Revolution* with the refrain '*But when you talk about destruction, don't you know that you can count me out*' told us that non-violent protest was the only way to speak your mind. The *White Album* reminded everyone that they were still the best damn rock band in the whole wide world.

Drug use skyrocketed, especially marijuana, the natural plant whose soft euphoric high provided the perfect escape. Enterprising hipsters traveled to Arizona and even Mexico to smuggle home Acapulco Gold, Panama Red, and Mexican Brown stuffed in spare tires, under seats, and behind car door panels. Venturing seekers experimented with LSD, DMT, peyote, and other hallucinogens to expand consciousness by encountering the effects of their mystic transcendence and accelerated learning, going from ordinary waking life to non-ordinary reality. The Grateful Dead's first financier and soundman Owsley Stanley, aka Bear, was the pied piper of the LSD revolution and credited with manufacturing over 5 million tabs of the drug.

In Robert Greenfield's biography, *Bear: The Life and Times of Augustus Owsley Stanley III*, the author writes that Owsley took 100 thousand hits of LSD that had been dyed and titled, *Monterey Purple*, to the pop festival. The Steely Dan song *Kid Charlemagne* was based in part on Owsley. Soft drug use soon gave way to harder drugs that led to increased social and health concerns.

The mecca for live music in Seattle was The Eagles Auditorium where the year began with Strawberry Alarm Clock and Crome Syrcus but then shifted to Grateful Dead and Quicksilver Messenger Service. The venue went on to host top-notch groups of the era that year. Chart topping bands such as Cream, Steppenwolf, The Doors, Iron Butterfly, and Deep Purple. When Pink Floyd appeared on August 10th a local journalist and music critic stated that, "the band provided mostly noise but not just plain noise, and we have too much noise in the world as it is." Vanilla Fudge from Long Island, NY also played along with Blue Cheer, a band that the same critic claimed, "were not much more than a hard rock band and that every major city in the country has at least a dozen of those." The auditorium also hosted Paul Butterfield, The Fugs, Country Joe & The Fish,

The Chambers Brothers, Moby Grape, The Steve Miller Band, Canned Heat, Youngbloods, Moody Blues, Chicago, Jeff Beck and a Draft Resistance Benefit on Oct. 6th. Popular local bands; Easy Chair, Floating Bridge, Crome Syrcus, Magic Fern, Fat Jack, and Juggernaut opened for many of the top bills.

Due to a city ordinance that prohibited juveniles from dancing, attendees of the shows sat on the floor until one night when the Grateful Dead's Jerry Garcia stepped to the microphone and said, "Vote no on politics and dance," which the kids gladly did. On The Dead's second night city inspectors arrived during *Turn on Your Love Light* and saw attendees on their feet dancing. They demanded that promoter Boyd Grafmyre stop the show and instruct the crowd to quit dancing, which he did. But after two songs the inspectors left and the crowd got back on their feet and pranced the night away.

The idea of Seattle's first underground newspaper occurred at the Free University in the U-District when local historian Paul Sawyer suggested to Paul Dorpat that, "What we need here is something like the *Berkeley Barb.*" His statement set in motion the beginnings of *Helix.*

Founded in 1967 by Paul Dorpat, Ray Collins, Lorenzo Milam, John Cunnick, Gary Eagle, and Tom Robbins, it soon included Walt Crowley, who claimed to be the first person to ever buy a copy. *Helix* was a collage of alternative rebellious politics, concert reviews, local happenings, colorful psychedelic graphics, sexuality, and articles promoting the burgeoning drug culture. It's first issue was published in March of 1967 and sold 2,500 copies. Readership climbed, within two months 12,000 copies sold, then 16,000 a month later. However, circulation dropped to 5,000 monthly after incidents of police harassment. The city was so threatened by the mere existence of the journal for spreading a new kind of ultra-liberal thinking in print that one man was arrested for selling the bi-weekly newspaper on a streetcorner. It folded after 124 issues in June of 1970, five weeks after the Kent State murders.

With *Helix* capturing the spirit of the local hippie movement Seattle radio did its part to promote the local and national music scene. Non-commercial KRAB-FM broadcast diversity to Seattle while KJR's disc jockey, concert promoter, and Founding Father of NW Rock-n-

Roll, Pat O'Day ruled the AM airwaves. In 1968 O'Day brought Jimi Hendrix back home for his first show and booked all his concerts around the country for that year with his company, Concerts West. If you were a teenager with a Philco or Westinghouse transistor radio that year, O'Day's daily radio program was the one to turn your dial to on 950 AM and his weekly Fab-50 play list allowed kids to keep up with current hits and popular music.

In Duvall, local musician and radio producer, Larry "Jug" Van Over, had recently heard a broadcast on KRAB-FM where they destroyed a piano by sledgehammer. Enlightened yet disappointed by the violent sound of the listening experience, Van Over mused to his friends that they should attempt the same thing but try for a more inspiring musical sound, suggesting that maybe they could drop a piano from a building, or better yet, a helicopter! Van Over soon requested help from Paul Dorpat at the *Helix* who suggested they could tack the idea onto a soon coming benefit titled, *Media Mash,* that Country Joe & The Fish were scheduled to play. Those who attended the concert got a free admission ticket to "The Drop." The idea came to fruition on

April 28, 1968 at Van Over's farm off the Cherry Valley Road.

The Generation Gap had been growing over the last number of years and the concept of a rock festival was fairly new to the country. The two-day Northern California Folk Rock Festival at the Santa Clara County Fairgrounds happened in May and future Woodstock entrepreneur Michael Lang helped stage The Miami Pop Festival at Gulfstream Park that same month. The Fantasy Fair in Marin County was in June, one week before the Monterey Pop Festival, which was a galvanizing moment in musical history, and the Newport Pop Festival at Costa Mesa, California, occurred in August, where flowers were dropped from helicopters on attendees.

But never had a festival occurred at a rural undeveloped site over a three-day period where bands played 12 to 18 hours a day to concert goers who stayed and camped at the venue with food and services provided. The Sky River Rock Festival, near the Skykomish River outside of Sultan, changed all that. It was a template of things to come and was empowered by a free-thinking visionary generation of like-minded people. They knew that peace and equality could rise to the surface and make real cultural change through the joy of music, lyrics, and true independence. The magic of that time still lingers and can be found; one just has to look for it.

Many things have been written and said about 1968 and the events that led up to that pivotal year when life and death, music, politics, culture, and social moral values were all thrown into the proverbial blender. The definition of being a non-conformist changed into someone who was a peace-loving person who wanted to leave both the normal world and social mores behind. But if we've learned anything over the years, we've learned that our struggles for basic unerring liberations and freedoms don't stop when a war or conflict ends.

I

Piano Drop

It was a glorious spring day. The sun shone brightly as the helicopter pilot went over his checklist then radioed the control tower for flight clearance. Larry stayed silent next to him as he fastened his seatbelt, then felt a touch of apprehension right when they got the a-okay and the chopper blades began to speed up. The noise was deafening. As the aircraft began to slowly rise above Boeing Field and the downtown skyline came into view, a wide grin came over his face.

"I love Seattle, especially on days like this," Harvey the pilot said as loudly as he could out of the corner of his mouth, "how about if we take a quick run over downtown before we head east?" In his mouth's other corner was a half-smoked unlit cigar, looking hapless.

"Sure," Larry answered as they headed north, then asked, "so, how long have you been flying these things?"

"For years, since Korea. The Army taught me how to fly a Bell just like this one. Hell, I flew them all, Chickasaw's, Hiller's, but we didn't fly 50-caliber gunships like they're doing now in Nam. We only did medical evacuations, getting our injured boys out," Harvey said, adjusting the old cigar in his mouth with his tongue, his voice like frayed sandpaper. Larry nodded as he nervously twisted in his seat.

When they flew past a new skyscraper being built Harvey joked, "I guess they're calling that thing the box the Space Needle came in." He laughed to himself just as the actual Needle came into view. Right then Jug felt a tingle in his teeth and gums. Gazing through the glass-bubbled windshield that encapsulated the cockpit, Larry watched as the Needle changed into mind massaging colors of dayglo patterns in blues and greens. Tie-dye flashes ran up and down the steel structure while the observation deck spun like a top. With that, he knew the half tab of windowpane acid he'd dropped an hour earlier during his ride in was taking effect, but at the same time he was relieved that the

Needle didn't melt. Signaling to him that he'd taken the proper dosage for the massive day ahead.

"Nice — view!" Larry forced out of his mouth over the loud, mind jarring noise of the chopper blades. The pilot nodded his head in reply as he moved the cyclic pitch and turned the aircraft east, towards their destination.

"So . . . you've done thing kind of thing before?"

"Oh, yeah," the pilot replied. "I've moved piano's this way a few times. In Korea I dropped small ordinance to clear out landing zones, but *never* have I dropped a piano."

"Oh, um, that's cool," Larry replied, not knowing how to respond to his Army days. He glanced over at him. His tan face became more wrinkled and weathered by the second. Then the cigar stub turned into a big fat wheat paper joint, Larry burst out laughing. Harvey gave him a questionable look.

As they passed over Woodinville, Larry noticed there were an awful lot of Sunday drivers out, far more than any other weekend. When they approached Duvall, the bridge into town looked like a one lane parking lot. Surprised, he directed the way so Harvey headed the chopper up the Cherry Valley Road. It was packed with bumper-to-bumper cars.

“I thought you said that there’d only be about 300 folks out here for this thing,” the airman said, his scratchy voice serious in a questioning manner. Larry smiled back, “I’ve never seen a traffic jam like this out here before. I had no idea it’d be this crowded.”

Nearing his farm and the drop zone, Larry pointed at the old upright piano he’d hauled out to his field and laid flat on its back next to a platform of decked timber, the intended target. Hundreds of people were gathered around it, all of them dressed in hippie garb. Women in granny dresses and beads stood with hirsute men in flannel shirts and patched over jeans milling around in wait. Others sat on blankets on the hill having picnics, making a day of it. Some sat on car hoods while others climbed trees for a better view.

Just then somebody blew into a police whistle, everybody within listening distance laughed like they owned the world. The stage, an open long-haul trailer had been brought in a week before and parked right next to Larry’s unfinished house. It was covered with band equipment; microphones, amplifiers and a PA system. Country Joe and The Fish were already playing *Not So Sweet Martha Lorriane* with its keyboard intro and rambling lead guitar. Some near the stage danced and sang along with Country Joe in hippie happiness while others waited patiently for the real show to begin.

Harvey hovered his chopper over the spectacle for a moment while the crowd looked up at them, hands held at their foreheads shielding the sun. Larry looked down too at the burgeoning flock, rife for an afternoon of fun, some throwing frisbee or hanging around in groups.

Seeing the enormous crowd at the landing site Harvey began his decent but hollered, “No way, no way, no way!”

“What exactly is your apprehension here?”

“They’re not going to get out of the way for the drop!” he answered, setting the chopper down next to the piano.

“They’ll move — man — they’ll moo . . . ove,” he relayed, then grinned, his head now swirling with acid. “Trust me, Harvey . . . it’ll be like the Red Sea all over again!”

“Okay, but they’ve got to give me plenty of room, or no drop,” the flyer barked, shaking his head as he let go of the controls. The band stopped playing and a voice came over the sound system instructing the throng.

“Stay back! Get away from the woodpile! Stay safe!”

“That’s Paul,” Larry said. “He’ll keep ‘em away.” As the crowd parted, Harvey and Larry jumped out. Larry ambled over to the spectators, his long hair flowing, his mind bending and swirling. He opened his arms to keep everyone away from the still spinning chopper blades while the pilot began to unload the haul line and hook up the harness to the piano. He took the cigar out of his mouth and motioned at Larry with it, beckoning him to assist.

“Here, help me loop the harness around it. Good thing you’ve already got it on its back, it’ll be more stable.” The joyful curious horde began to drift over to them.

“Oh, man, this is so out-a-sight,” said a scruffy longhaired fellow in faded blue jeans as he wiped the hair away from his eyes. His buddy held out a lit joint to Larry, but he turned it down, saying, “Thanks — man, but I’m doin’ fine." Near them a fellow was waving a white flag with a peace sign on it as some firecrackers were shot off.

"Far out! That thing is gonna go kaboom when it hits those logs," one fellow remarked in stoned bliss.

"Man, that piano will explode like a musical bomb."

"Yeah, cool man, like no song you've ever heard before! It'll be a power chord for the heavens."

"No shit, like in the key of B for bomb, brother, no doubt."

"It'll be like the final piano chord in *Day in The Life*!"

"Right on dude! Just like that! Like the end of the world!"

Harvey and Larry got back in the helicopter and the pilot began his assent, the slack in the cable went taught. The chopper lurched forward when the piano lifted off the ground, swaying. Some of the crowd stood back while others ran up to gather on the hillside, joining their new found friends, most of them drinking beer and smoking weed, cheering with delight as they watched the piano take flight and rise into the sky. Harvey performed a slow circle so he could get his bearings and navigate towards the intended target, making calculations.

He glanced around nervously, making sure that no one was near the woodpile and at a safe distance. Larry's heart pounded with excitement as he told himself. *It's happening, man! It's really fucking happening!*

When they were about 60 feet above the landing site Harvey slowed the helicopter down to an eventual halt right over the woodpile, but the piano kept moving forward, it in turn dragged the small chopper ahead causing it to wobble and Harvey panicked. He hit the release, but the piano stubbornly refused, it didn't let go.

"Shit!" Harvey spat, "the damn thing is too heavy, 'er, maybe something's caught down there?" Then he tried the emergency release and the helicopter shot upward.

"There she goes!" Harvey hollered with relief, and delight, looking downward at the 500 pound upright piano fall.

Larry leaned out his window too, and watched as his cheap St. Vincent DePaul instrument drop towards the ground.

Everyone at first held their breath then gasped as they watched the piano arc its way through the air, but then it landed in between the woodpile and the crowd.

With an unexpected — thump — the poor old piano came back to earth landing in the soft grass of Larry's field, cracking in half. The anticipated key of B not realized, the chord for the heavens never heard, yet the collective mantra, "Far Out!" filled the air as the onlookers screamed with heavenly joy at the sight.

A rush of hippies instantly descended upon the helpless wreckage and began to tear it apart. First the legs were busted off with the swift kick of a boot, then the top lid was ripped away, the side boards were next and so on until the whole thing was consumed by a thirsty crowd of souvenir seekers. By the time Larry was back on terra firma and at the site nothing was left of it. He saw two hippies carrying the soundboard up the hill. There wasn't even a felt hammer or ivory key for a keepsake.

The band started playing again and as Larry began to climb the hill the sound of Country Joe singing, *Janis*, the words slipped into his ears like jello. *Something about how all she wants to do is get stoned on booze and then you have to watch her die.* It was a fitting end.

Through a haze of pot smoke Larry headed through the crowd. People cheered and patted him on the back, then he saw Paul and a few friends. He walked over to them. Paul smiled brightly and announced, "Well, well, well, if it isn't the Flying Dutchman!" Everyone laughed, including Larry.

"Boy," he gasped, "they sure devoured that thing. That piano is history! And here I didn't even get a piece of it. Can you believe that?"

"Oh, I believe it," Paul replied, grinning widely at his friend and then embraced him, saying, "Well, it was still a great success. We may not have gotten the sound we were searching for, but it still turned out to be a damn fine day! Don't you think so, Jug?"

"Yeah, you're right compadre," Larry replied, "a good effort was made by all. So, how about we go get us a beer?"

Paul nodded in agreement. As they trudged off for a cold one a lone hippie walked by them and said, “Hey man, that was awesome. Let’s do it again sometime.”

Hours later after the crowd had all cleared-out Larry, Paul, and a few assorted friends sat around a campfire, some cooking hotdogs or marshmallows on the end of sticks, the magic of the day still lingering in the night air. Ancient tribal instincts had been realized and everyone basked in the holy sacrament of the current times, they had won the day. With dank, organic smoke rising straight up, the fires glow and warmth feeding their souls, their freak flags flew proud with the prospects of a special point in time. Larry picked softly on his mandolin, then stopped and ran his fingers across his receding hairline, looked up at the stars and started to reflect.

“Harvey, our pilot today, was a Korean war vet, good guy. He was funny too. When we first took off, he went north over downtown Seattle, but when we got to the Space Needle, that’s when the acid hit and boy did it! The Needle turned all these bright colors, dayglo and such, and then the top of it started spinning," he said laughing, holding his arms out, the mandolin neck in one hand, "man it was so far out! He had no idea I was peaking." Everyone howled with gaiety. Once the laughter died down Jug continued. "And then, when we got here and he saw the carpet of humanity below us he wasn't gonna do it. He didn't think they'd get out of the way. But I talked him into it. Told him they'd part like the Red Sea. I mean after all, it was a biblical event! One to rejoice in the heavens!"

Everyone buckled over with laughter, Jug started picking his mandolin again, but a little faster this time. After a few bars he stopped playing then looked around his circle of close friends, he had an idea.

"So, I think we should try to do that again, but in a different format. We'd still need to have music, it's just that, it feels like everyone today is looking for more."

"Exactly," Paul responded, "more music and more fun."

"Yeah, but how? How can we present something unique?"

"If 3,000 people came to hear one band, for a piano drop," Paul wondered out loud, "how many would come to hear a dozen, or even two dozen bands?"

"Right!" Tim exclaimed. "Just like Monterey last summer."

"Sure, sure," Paul agreed, "maybe do it over a few days and have all kinds of groups. Rock, blues, bluegrass, folk. Shit, if they could do Monterey down there, then why the hell can't we do the same thing up here?"

"Right!" Larry said loudly, jumping to his feet and pointing at Paul. "Right, right, right! If they can do it so, can we! But we've got to offer more than music."

The group looked up at him, their eyes all sparking with excitement, knowing they were on to something. Larry stroked his handlebar moustache, they could see his brain was churning with colossal thoughts as he walked around the group, the flames licking at the night.

"How 'bout we do a music festival, like over a couple of days just like Monterey but different, you know, the same, but different. Like maybe we have camping and all the concert goers stay and we have vendors selling food."

"Brilliant!"

"Excellent!" We'll get Hendrix to lite his guitar on fire again!"

"Right! And maybe have The Who wreck all their equipment, too! But we've got to offer more than what we just did with the piano, there's got to be something else that will get everyone's attention. Something big, something bigger than big. Like, um, carnival rides or, I just can't put my finger on it just yet. Something grand."

"Yeah, but if we get top-notch bands that folks know about, that in itself will get everyone to come," Gary countered.

"Yes," Larry replied, "but we need a gimmick and a catchy name and a knock-out location. Like in a big old cow pasture or on a river, or a lake, at a natural setting. Wait! I think I've got it. I can see it now. Instead of carnival rides we can offer hot air ballon rides! That's it! That's it!"

"What are you talking about, Van Over?" Tim said, laughing out loud, "that's silly. How are you gonna to do that?"

"And where on earth are you going to get a hot air balloon?"

"Yeah, enlighten us, Larry. How would that work?"

"I'm not sure yet," he replied, "we couldn't do it like normal balloon rides where a balloon flies away with its riders and then a car chases it down. It could be just an up and down thing, you know, keep it tied down with sturdy ropes and the riders would go up like fifty feet and then be pulled back down. Or wait, wait, we could fill the balloon with just enough hot air that it wouldn't take off and a rider could be like weightless and spring off the ground like ten-feet and land again. That would be so cool. Don't you think? I mean people would love that, to feel what it's like to be weightless. Right?"

"Oh, for Christ sakes Larry, that's insane, it's madness."

"Don't worry, I'll figure it out. I'm telling ya it'll work."

"Okay, if you say so," Gary chuckled. "We need to start planning this thing. Having live music on a river is a great idea and I know for sure that part will work. This could be epic on a grand scale. We could make history."

II

Universal Mother

Summer was setting in, the 4th of July was done and gone, Johnson was still in the White House, but not for long, and *Jumpin' Jack Flash* battled it out with *Mrs. Robinson* over the airwaves. The driver had his radio on Seattle's KJR; they were in the middle of a promo. *"Pat O'Day here, live from the Jet City. Today we've got Jerry Kaye from WCFL —"*

He abruptly turned the dial, changing the channel to KOL-FM, *You Keep Me Hangin' On* by Vanilla Fudge blared out of the tiny dash speaker as he turned off Highway 203 and onto the Ben Howard Road.

Glancing at the envelope for its return address, he slowly made his way through the lush countryside past farms, cottage homes, and green fields of bovine and croplands. Finally, he found the correct mailbox and turned his car up a gravel driveway lined by a forest of thick trees. He parked in front of a small farmhouse with a covered porch that was sided with cedar shakes, a hand-pumped water well sat in front of the place, the red paint on its handle worn off.

Outbuildings and well-tended berry trellises surrounded him, a few chickens were about, clucking and scratching at the ground while the faint guitar strains of *White Rabbit* seeped out of the home like liquid hookah smoke. As he stepped away from his car a dark-haired barefooted woman came out of the house, followed by a strutting rooster with black tailfeathers and two hens. She casually waved and then walked over to him. The woman looked to be in her late 30s, mid-length dark hair and wore a pair of frayed white cut-offs. With the music and string of beads hanging from her neck, he knew she was a free spirit and absolutely the perfect type of land owner he was looking for.

"I'm guessing you're John," she said, touching her black framed glasses. "I got your reply letter two days ago."

"Yes," he answered, smiling, walking over to her. They shook hands as he held up the letter she'd mailed to the *Helix* more than a week before.

"I'm John Chambless. I'm really glad you answered our ad. This is a great place."

"Oh, thanks. I'm Betty Nelson, but I go by Ma Kahuna, or just Ma. So, um, John," she said with a touch of apprehension, then crossed her arms and started tapping a foot. "I've got a working farm here. Horses, pigs, seventy-some chickens, and lots of berries. I don't want to see any of that being wrecked or disturbed."

"Okay, I understand, we'll do the best we can. You just tell us what you want as far as protecting it all. We'll have a security team around the clock to watch things."

"Good. I like the sound of that. But I can do my part too, I guess. I'll keep the chickens caged and the barn doors shut. But tell me, have you done anything like this before?"

"Yes, I have. For the last two years I've been the musical director of the Berkeley Folk Festival, so I've done this kind of thing before. And we won't allow anyone to wreck anything."

"Okay. And what's your relationship with the *Helix*?" she asked, stiffly. "I mean. Don't get me wrong. I love it, buy a copy every chance I get."

"Oh, I know the folks that run it, they're good people."

"So, is the *Helix* putting this thing on? You work for them?"

"Oh no, I don't work for the *Helix*. I'm a philosophy professor at the University of Washington." When he said that, Ma's body language instantly changed. "I would call them partners. They'll be running ads, helping out, and their printer will do the tickets. Myself and a friend of mine, Cyrus Noe, are financing the project. Both of us have mortgaged our homes to put this festival on. We have forty-thousand dollars of seed money that we've raised for it."

"Wow, that's a lot of money and very good of you and all. But um, who is going to profit from this? Are you and Cyrus gonna make money?"

"No one, not me, not Cy, nobody except the musicians will profit from this," John answered quickly. "We have a non-profit organization, The New American Community that we've created to distribute any profits we make to Native American Organizations. The *Helix* won't make any money off this. That's why we'd like to see if you'd be interested in not charging us for the use of your property for well, weeks, maybe more. We'll need lots of time to set up everything, and then tear it all down and clean-up."

"Hmm, that's unusual. This non-profit is, um, legit?"

"Oh yes, absolutely, we aren't looking to have some sort of big blow-out event. It will be on a small scale."

"I see," Betty said, "and what kind of music will you have?"

"Mostly local groups from Seattle, if we can afford a headliner or two, we'll do that. But we'd like to offer a wide array of musical styles, like folk and rock, some bluegrass, and the blues. Acoustic songwriters."

"Okay, I like the sound of that. How about if I show you around?"

"I'd like that. I need to get an idea for how we'd set up."

She led him over to a good-sized level area at the base of a gentle slope. John knew right away that it would be an excellent location for a large stage. He stopped and looked around, she did too and put her hands on her hips.

"This really is the ideal venue for an outdoor music festival," John said, believing he'd found the perfect match.

"It is. I know. That's why I answered the ad," Ma said, smiling. John looked over the property again.

"This level area is what, maybe 4 or 5 acres and the gentle slope is like a natural amphitheater," John replied, grinning, gesturing upward with his hand.

"I've got about 40 total acres and 18 of it in pasture."

"Your place is awesome. We'd like to offer some food items and have vendors for that, we'd provide Sanikans too. Basic services. What about water, I noticed your hand pumped well that could provide some water, maybe we could set up a main water source?"

Betty's eyes got big and she motioned for John to follow her. "Over here I've got a natural spring."

"Great."

They stood at the spring and looked down on it. The flowing water slowly gurgling up out of the ground. It spread out over the immediate area then ran towards the forest and county road below in a small mud-lined channel.

"Okay," John mused, "I'm not sure if that would provide enough water for a few thousand people."

"Oh gosh. You know, I've got a friend who's been bugging me about developing it better. He thinks he can use a small stick of dynamite to get it to flow more."

"Really?"

"Yep. I'd be glad to get ahold of him, have him try it for you."

"That would be great. We'd be happy to pay his fee."

"Also, like I mentioned in my letter, I don't have

a phone and there's only a small fuse box at the house for my fridge and some lights. There's not even close to enough power to run a bands equipment here."

"Alright, well. We'll need to rent an industrial generator in that case for the PA and amplifiers. We'll need to locate a place for it. And as far as not having a phone," John said, scratching his head, "I think we'll be able to get around that, somehow."

For the next half-hour they hiked Ma Kahuna's property, the whole time John was laying out in his mind's eye where everything would go. Her pasture had a gentle natural slope that slowly ascended from where a stage could be built, it was surrounded by a thick forest that made a perfect amphitheater. The stage area was somewhat close to the county road and there was a small natural bench of ground where a generator could be placed between the road and the stage site.

Pointing, John said, "That spot there just above the county road would work for a generator. It's close to your driveway and a stage location. We'd have to do a small amount of brush clearing and cut the bank a little, by hand of course with shovels. You'd have the final say on everything. I think it would work. Plus, the carpentry crew would probably want to stay out here, camp out you know, while they set up. And most of the festival attendees will camp out, if that's alright with you?"

"Camping's fine but I don't want anyone tearing down my fencing for firewood," Betty said, sternly, then motioned, "that little level area would be fine with me for your generator and if the stage crew wants to camp here then I would absolutely welcome that. It'd be fun."

"We'll make absolutely sure that no one tears anything apart for firewood. I promise."

"Good, thank you," Betty replied, nodding.

They continued walking, John noticed that the ground was soft and a bit moist, which was concerning to him. Her long lines of multiple raspberry plants were, too.

"Does it rain more out here than it does in Seattle?"

"Oh, maybe. We had lots of the stuff in June. But everyone knows summer doesn't arrive until after the 4th of July. It'll be dry from now till the end of September."

"Really?"

"Yes, you and the festival should be fine," she answered knowingly.

"Alright, it's just that. I can see problems if it rains."

"Problems?"

"Well, yes. If the weather doesn't cooperate and we get rain the ground will soften and then turn to mud and if that happens, we may have difficulty with hauling band equipment to and from the stage, you see."

"It won't, trust me. All of August and the rest of summer will be dry. It always is, I know it will be."

"Okay, if you say so. What about all your raspberry plantings? Also, I'm a little concerned about parking."

"My raspberry harvest will be over by then. But why worry about parking? People can just park anywhere they can, on the side of the road."

"Gosh, I don't think the county sheriff would like that. We're going to try and find a parking location or two along the highway in town and then shuttle people."

"Well," Betty said, "that would be good but I still think people will park out here on the road."

"Yes, I'm sure they will but having a parking lot in Sultan would be the best way to go. So, Betty, Ma I mean, do we have a deal? Will you let us use your place?"

"Absolutely!"

"Fantastic. But we will need to start building a stage and getting the generator site developed quickly. The whole set up will take a long time. Weeks and weeks. Are you okay with that?"

"Yes. You can get going as soon as you'd like."

"Alright then. I'll mail you a no-fee lease agreement that begins right away and runs through say, September 15th. That will give us enough time to build a stage and bring in everything and do the clean-up. Plus, we'll buy a liability insurance policy to protect both you and us in case of any mishaps or accidents."

III

The Newsroom

I was being too meticulous with word selection again. Late on deadline and thinking too much, I pecked away at the keys on the typewriter. The long bending ash on the cigarette in my mouth finally broke free, landing in my lap. Not yet ready to leave my train of thought, I let it lay so I could dash-off my article before quitting time. Once the paragraph was finished, I looked down and brushed off my slacks.

Crap, what a mess. I've always tried my best to look good at work. Ironed shirt and trousers, suit coat and tie, shoes polished, and all of it to keep my boss, Fred Corson happy — even though I can't stand the guy. Today, like every day, I recognized the sound of his hard-soled shoes slapping against the floor coming down the newsroom aisle, resounding above all the other long-time reporters grinding out daily grist for Tacoma readers. I looked up, stared at him and forced a smile, just like always.

“McCalister!” he screeched, taking the cigar out of his mouth, his protruding belly folding down over his unseen belt. “I’ve got a new assignment for you.”

“But I haven’t finished this one on the city council meeting —”

“That can wait. I’ve got a big story out in Sultan, and I need you to cover it right away. I just found out that the advertising department has already ran a few ads for them. I didn’t know a thing about it and KIRO-TV has been reporting on it all week. Phil in the media archive has saved some of it. Come on,” Corson said gesturing, “I’ll have him show you some of the footage.”

“Sultan? Really?” I asked getting up, following him.

“Yes, it’s way up on US 2,” Fred replied, his stiff

wingtips echoing down the hall. "There's a meeting this evening about some music event that the locals are trying to shut down. So, I want you up there to get the skinny." *The skinny. That's what he said when he really meant the facts, the real bricks and mortar to a story.*

"A musical event? You mean like at the high school?"

"No, Cliff!" Fred snapped, walking into the media room where the archivist sat in front of a monitor. The place was a cluttered mess, desks covered with files and over-loaded boxes crammed full of ledgers and binders, and a long aisle of metal shelving filled to the bejesus with ancient editions and weekend magazines. "It's a hippie live music thing — since our regular art critic is gone on vacation and you're my youngest reporter you get the job. I want a full-blown feature article on it. The big time!" He turned to Phil and said, "Bring up that KIRO reporting on that hippie thing you showed me out in Sultan."

"When did we start writing articles from TV reporting?"

Fred exhaled and said, "Son, I've been at this a long time and when we're in a jam and we don't have a reporter available to cover an event, well then, we do what we can. Besides, we're both in the news business and I'm sure they read us as much as we watch them."

"Okay, so, this is like a concert thing, then," I asked as Phil worked at getting the footage up on the video tape machine.

"They're calling it a rock festival," Corson said, bending over and staring at the screen, "and I want you to see some of this reporting before you head out." He turned his head back at me then quipped, "Just watch and learn."

A TV reporter in a suit stood in front of a large stage under construction as workers walked back and forth behind him. Evergreens stood tall as a backdrop and the site looked rural. When one long-haired fellow in jeans and a white T-shirt walked by, the reporter flagged him down and asked, "Could I get a minute? What's your role here? Are you friends of the landowner?"

"Oh, hi, yes. We're all friends here," he said with bright eyes, flashing a guru grin. "I'm helping build the stage, and doing other things, but now — I'm eating a hotdog," the hippie said, then chomped down on his lunch with gusto.

"As you can see, everybody here at Betty Nelson's Raspberry Farm is working hard to get her property ready for the Sky River Rock Festival next Labor Day weekend."

"Okay!" Corson said, standing up. "So, if KIRO thinks they can get away with shoddy reporting like that then I've seen it all. Give me a break, I mean, do they really think they can put some hippie kid on TV eating a hotdog and call it news? Well, I say hogwash!" he vented, gnawing on his cigar. "Your writing is far superior than that excuse for an on-air segment. That is lousy reporting if I've ever seen it, and I know you can do better because you write damn good copy. I want an in-depth article on it. You got that, McCalister?"

"I guess I do, but why is everyone so obsessed with all these hippies?"

Fred shook his head and then glared at me. He rolled his eyes and replied, "Because the public is asking for it, that's why. The news every night is filled with hippies these days, ever since last summer in San Francisco. But I want you to dig deep into the real stuff of what's driving these kids today. You need to grasp their concept and try to figure out this whole damn thing. Get the real skinny."

"I'm sorry, Fred. I'm big on jazz and follow some of the rock music these days. I've got a couple of Beatles records and I'll try my best. But I don't really know or understand anything about hippies."

"Nobody understands them, that's the point. I sure as hell don't."

"It just seems like this is all such a waste of time."

"McCalister," Corson belched, "I am sending you to cover this thing and I don't want to hear anymore bellyaching. Now get going. I want 1,200 words about this meeting tonight on my desk Monday morning! And, I want you to cover the whole thing, start to finish, so you'll need to be up there again in a week to begin full coverage. I'll pay for it all, keep your receipts and I'll get Margaret to issue you a company credit card." Fred turned around and headed out of the room. I did the same and watched his fat ass waddle away. At the desk, I picked up my briefcase with a long sigh and headed out feeling defeated.

Why me? And why a live music hippie thing? What's that supposed to be? Christ I'm never gonna get ahead around here. I should have stayed in Spokane where there was normal news.

I needed gas up so I stopped at the Richfield on the way out of town. The attendant at the station looked young, like he'd dropped out of school kind of young. Bushy hair, glasses, worn out tennis shoes, but an honest face. *Hmm, maybe he knows about the Sultan thing.*

"Hey buddy," I said, rolling down my window. "Fill 'er up with regular."

"Okay," the attendant said, "what year's your Impala?"

"It's a '59. Do you happen to know how to get to Sultan?"

"Sure, sure," he replied, stuffing a rag into his back pocket. "Go north on the freeway to Everett then take a right on US 2. It's about a half hour from there — yeah, I always get confused between the '59 and the '60."

"I know. The body styles are similar and easy to confuse." I handed him two dollars for the fill-up and then asked, "You hear about some rock party up there over Labor Day?"

"I have. Heard about it on the radio. They're havin' a rock festival, not a rock party. Live music for 3 days, I've been savin' up. It's like six bucks for the weekend."

"Alright, thanks, maybe I'll see you there." I pulled out of the station and headed for the freeway onramp then turned north on a desolate road. The sky held no promise; it was one of those typical northwest days. Banks of gray and white clouds hung low in the sky, like mashed potatoes mixed with a dash of hazy gravy smoke blotting out the late summer sunshine.

The farther I headed north the more the piles of clouds attempted to gang up on each other, rubbing each other the wrong way, just like Fred and my job. It made me feel like an insignificant bug trapped under an inverted cereal bowl. *Geez, everything is dull and boring here. I don't feel like doing this. What do I care about some hippie thing out in the middle of nowhere. Just my luck. Now all of next weekend is shot, and what the heck is there in Snohomish County anyway? Just a bunch of chainsaw hillbilly's and moonshiners living in cabins out in the tick-infested woods, or maybe in caves.*

The further I drove the more I missed Spokane, my folks, and the house on South Hill with its creaky floors, ornate fixtures, and clawfoot bathtubs. *That old place had a lot of charm; it still does. I need to go back and visit the folks more often. Maybe after Labor Day?*

I missed my Gonzaga friends, too. Sam Perkins and Carl Victor. I loved drinking way too much beer with those guys at Joey's till midnight, eating cheesy pizza and playing pool, smoking. If they lived here, we'd probably be in the tavern every other night. *I need to get back there for some vacation time, maybe next summer, play some golf. If you miss it so much maybe you should just move back there. Yeah, well, I don't know. Jesus, Cliff, quit fretting so much. You're pitiful. You need something new in your life and soon, like right away.*

IV

Town Hall

At Everett I had to roll up my window, the effluvial stench of pulp mills filled the cab with the most horrible of smells. It was such an alien stink that even my well-trained olfactory nerves, which had built up a Tacoma tolerance to the awfulness of industrial smells, was overcome with sinus rejection.

Nauseated, I followed the US 2 sign and headed east over a high steel bridge painted drab green, the rusty bolts standing out like warts. Once over the river the road proceeded across an elevated two-lane rickety trestle that appeared to be old and in disrepair. It made me nervous. I opened the wing window and carefully lit a Winston, the smoke instantly calmed me down, the vile scent of pulp gone.

Once across the trestle the countryside was rich with brilliant green pastures and acreage, mostly tall corn still growing, the tassels on the stalks bending over, full of pollen. Then strings of dairy farms with silos where large white barns rested beside holstein dotted fields and hard-working farmers on red tractors were cutting green chop for their herd.

After over two hours on the road, I finally got to Sultan and found the town hall. There were all kinds of folks milling around outside, most of them older and in work clothes. At the top of the wide long staircase the meeting room was packed, standing room only and nobody seemed to be smiling, nothing but frowns and lots of lively conversation. There were well over a hundred people there. Men in red suspenders that had white lettering on them, Oregon Chain, Stihl, or Timber Beast. A few of them had tan fur-like pads fastened to their suspenders on one shoulder but nearly all of them were wearing soft leather moccasins. I was standing in the back with my notebook and pen ready to record an account when a gentleman walked slowly with a slight limp up to the podium with a stern look and a tight jaw. Once there, he picked up a gavel and struck it repeatedly against the sounding block to get everyone's attention.

"Quiet down please! Can we have some silence!" he loudly said, then waited. When the room was calm, he began. "Okay, thank you. Good evening, everybody. I know a lot of you have questions and concerns about the rock festival that's planned so we've got Snohomish attorney Frank Carr here to talk about what we can do to stop this thing from happening. Frank, can you come up here?" A man in a black suit who looked to be around 50 walked up to the front and stood next to the mayor.

"Thank you, Mayor Van Trojen," he said, looking tired. His gray hair was uncombed and his suit and tie were rumpled. "As most of you know, some of you have retained me to look into this rock show and I've found that there are no legal means to prevent this festival from happening."

Instantly a number of who I guess were loggers by their work clothes jumped to their feet groaning and motioning at him. One man loudly said, "We could have twenty-thousand of them hippies here smoking marijuana and threatening our kids, and trespassing, they're just a bunch of vagrants! You need to stop this thing!" Most of the crowd cheered when another fellow spoke up, "And where're they all supposed to park? That is if they even have cars! I don't even think any of them have jobs or work for a living. Bums all of them," a man said as I started jotting down some notes.

The mayor raised his hand for calm, then said, "So far, the event has been in no violation of any statute, but if any violations occur then the law will be enforced. I have Sheriff Jennings' full commitment on that."

"Okay, but what about food and facilities? We don't need a bunch of hippies wandering around town begging for food or, worse yet, stealing from the markets!"

"Yeah! Hippies are terrible, they don't have any money! Or any decency! This whole peace and love thing is for the birds. I say we end the thing right now!"

"Hold on, hold on," the mayor responded, looking flustered, "the organizers have a lawful permit and like Mr. Carr says, there is no legal means to stop it from happening. These people so far have done no harm to anybody. Until they do, their rights should be protected."

"What about that poster they have with a frog smoking a marijuana cigarette? They're advocating drug use!"

Many in the crowd vocally agreed when a heavy-set man with a dark, neatly trimmed beard raised his hand and began walking towards the podium. He had a professional look about him, slacks, white collared shirt, and confident stride. Once he got to the front of the hall, he said something quietly to the mayor as a hush fell over the room. After the mayor and him exchanged pleasantries, the fellow stepped to the podium and began speaking to the boisterous group.

"Good evening. I'm Cyrus Noe and the general manager of the festival. I wanted to address the concern you have over the artwork on one of the many posters that have been circulating and make it perfectly clear that I did not authorize that particular poster. However, I'd like to assure you that the marijuana cigarette you're referring to is merely a fine American cigar, nothing more and nothing less."

"Oh, for heavens sakes! We know that's not a cigar."

"Yeah, we ain't dumb mister. We know that's a

joint."

Cyrus continued in a calm manner. "There is no intention of advocating drugs. This festival is a musical event meant for all ages and we would never encourage any type of drug use."

"Right! And how are you going to stop all these hippies from smoking marijuana? We all know that stuff just leads to more serious problems, like heroin addiction." The crowd became more vocal so Cyrus raised his hands to help placate the crowd. He cleared his throat and began again with the voice of a diplomat.

"We will be doing our level best to not allow any drug use at all next weekend. You have my word on it. I will do my very foremost to deter any open use of illegal substances, I promise," he finished, stepping back from the podium.

"And what about the traffic and parking? How's that gonna be handled?" asked a man in a black and white work shirt.

The mayor glanced over at Mr. Noe so Cyrus stepped back to the podium. "We've contracted with local berry farmers to use their empty pastures for parking and shuttle services for festival goers. The farmers will be using their employee buses to take people to and from the event."

"Well, I say we all get our tractors out the day it starts and block the Ben Howard Road!" cracked a man in dirty overalls as he pushed his orange hat up on his forehead.

"Now, now," the mayor replied, back at the lectern. "That would be illegal and the sheriff's deputy would stop you from trying to stop them. They have a permit and all we can do now is try to work with them and help make it better, for us. It's all we can do. Cyrus and his group are doing a good job of coordinating all aspects."

"Work with them? Why?" A woman in a plaid dress with her hair in a beehive blurted, "the heck we're going to work with a bunch of hippie drop-outs! Why are we paying for a lawyer when he says he can't do anything?"

"Okay, Helen, I understand," Mayor Van Trojen said, "I know we're all frustrated with the situation, but —"

"That's it," she snapped, then stood up abruptly. "Dear Lord help us all. I've had enough of this."

With that everyone got up from their chairs and began to file out of the hall. I approached the podium and made eye-contact with the mayor then raised my hand to get his attention.

“Mayor? Could I get a word? I’ve got a few questions?”

“Um, yes, I suppose I could, and you might be?”

“Cliff McCalister, Tacoma News Tribune, sir,” I replied, reaching out to shake his hand. “I won’t take much of your time. I was wondering, for our readers, do you really expect up to, what was it, twenty-thousand people?” I asked, pen and notebook at the ready.

“Please, call me John. Well, Cliff, I spoke with the music director, a Mr. Chambless, of the festival just yesterday and they’ve already sold over nine-thousand tickets.”

“Wow, and the festival is still a week away, that’s big.”

“I know and the community is, well, as you could see, they’re not really taking it very well, some are, apprehensive.”

"I can understand and don't really know much about hippies either but in any event, I'm going to be covering the festival from start to finish," I said, handing him a business card. "Here's my work number, that is, if you need to get ahold of me. Please let me know if anything out of the ordinary happens this coming week."

"I will, good to meet you, Cliff. Call city hall if you need anything."

"Okay, thanks John. Oh, I'll need to find a motel for that weekend. Can you point me in the direction of one?"

"Sure, just head east up Main Street and you'll see the Dutch Cup Motel. Clean rooms, they've got a cafe, too."

"Very good, thank you, I'll go check it out. Good-bye."

Outside I looked for Mr. Noe to maybe ask him a question or two but didn't see him anywhere. *I'll try to talk with him at the festival.* Once in the Impala I drove up the street and found the motel. Inside the office, a woman was on the phone, talking loudly, seeming upset. She looked to be in her 40s, had auburn hair that was in a bun and stood behind a tall counter.

When she was done talking, she looked at me and sighed.

"It's been a long day. I'm Bonnie, how can I help you?"

"Well, I wanted to see about a room for the Labor Day weekend. Friday through Monday night, so four nights."

"This is your lucky day. The fellow on the phone just canceled and that's my only room. This hippie thing has got us busier than we've been in a long time."

"Great! Good timing, I'll take it," I said, but to myself I thought. *Well, you're stuck with this assignment now.*

"Will that be cash or charge?" she asked, smiling brightly. I reached for my wallet and handed the company card to her. She quickly placed it on the imprinter, ran it through, had me sign it, then pulled off the receipt. It was for $25.08.

"You'll be in room 24 on the main level in the middle. And my husband, Don, he runs the café kitchen."

"Thanks, I'll see you both soon. Oh, I drove up today from Tacoma but I went up to Everett first then came out US 2. Is there a quicker way to Tacoma?"

Bonnie grinned and pointed west, then directed, "Go back to Monroe and take a left to Duvall, follow that until you hit Snoqualmie and take Highway 18 west. That will save you a lot of miles and remember, check-in is at two-o'clock, but absolutely no sooner. We run a tight ship here at the Cup, there's no funny business."

She gave me a wry grin as I turned and left. *Geez. I'm ready for this whole thing to be over before it even begins.*

V

The Apartment

An hour and a half later I was back at home at 6th and Saint Helens in Tacoma, dead tired and downtrodden. Just as I slipped the key into the deadbolt my neighbor's doorknob turned and its door jerked open, the chain snapping back hard, holding its progress.

"I thought I heard something," the neighbor lady said.

"Oh, hi there, Mrs. Richardson. It's just me, Cliff," I replied, trying not to roll my eyes.

"Why, you're home late. I thought you were a prowler."

"Nope, no burglar here. Good to see you," I

answered, opening the lock, cracking the door, taking a half-step inside —

“Say, Cliff, could you help me tomorrow morning? I’ve got some big heavy boxes that I need put up on a closet shelf.”

“Sure, sure. I’ll knock sometime late tomorrow morning.”

“Thank you, Cliff. You’re such a sweet young man.”

Just then the phone rang, saving me. I had a good idea who it was. “Okay, gotta go, see you tomorrow.”

Walking into the sparsely furnished flat of bare white walls, matted down wool carpet, boxes and shelves of books, magazines, record player, album collection, and tiny kitchen. I got to the telephone just in time and grabbed the receiver off the wall mounted unit on the fifth ring in a worn-out huff.

“Hello.”

“Clifford, it’s Mom. How are you doing? I called earlier.”

"Oh, hi Mom. Things are good. I had a really long day."

"You still miss Spokane, don't you? I can hear it in your voice."

"Yeah, I suppose I do. How're you and Dad doing?"

"Oh, we're good. So, listen, we've decided to have your aunt and uncle over next weekend. You need to come over for it. You haven't seen them in a while and they want —"

"I can't, the newspaper has me working that weekend, even on Labor Day."

"You're working? On Labor Day? Nobody works on Labor Day. Why on earth does that paper have you working?"

"It's an assignment to do a feature on a music festival."

"A music festival. On Labor Day? Good grief. But we haven't seen you in ages. Are you making this up?"

"No Mom, I'm not. I have to work. I'm sorry."

"Okay, but everyone was hoping to see you."

"Tell them hi for me and I'll try to get over soon."

"Alright. Please call us next week. We sure wish you were working for the Spokesman Review. It's such a wonderful paper."

"I know Mom. So, um, I have to go. I'm going to start packing, plus I have an article to finish by Monday."

"Okay bye. I love you."

"Bye, Mom. Love you, too."

I hung up shaking my head, then wished the next weekend had already come and gone while setting my briefcase down on the desk, aka: the dining room table. The black and gold Royal Eldorado typewriter and piles of paperwork sat waiting for me. Files, old articles I'd written, pens, bottle of wite-out, overflowing ashtray, mail, and a few books that I hadn't gotten to reading yet.

In the kitchen the fridge held few items; a half-gallon of milk, three Heidelberg's, butter, eggs, one piece of dried out pizza and a saucepan half full of soup from two-nights before. In the freezer, Swanson's TV Dinners, one turkey, the other Salisbury Steak. Instead of cooking, I opened a bottle of beer and took a long drink.

I automatically stepped over to my records and started flipping through them. Coltrane, Monk, Billie Holiday, then pulled out my favorite, *Sketches of Spain* by Miles Davis. I cued it up on the Montclair, then flopped on the couch and tried to relax.

On the coffee table sat another cigarette butt filled ashtray, and an open pack of Winston's. *I need to cut back on those things*. The Greek Mythology book my aunt gave me a year ago for Christmas was still waiting to be read, it'd been sitting there ever since. Thinking of her, I picked it up and thumbed through the colorful, shiny pages. Athena, the goddess of wisdom. O*h, she's smart I bet.* Aphrodite, the goddess of love and lust, *Man, she's a babe.* Dionysus, the god of wine, *I like him.* Hermes, the protector of travelers and orators, *Hmm, that's interesting.* And Pan, the God of the wild, shepherds, flocks and rustic music, fields, and wooden glens.

Geez, that's really interesting! Rustic music, fields and woods. They all *. . . sound like . . . where I'm going to be . . .* zz *. . . next . . .* zzzzz *. . . weekend —*

☼

Filtered morning sunshine did its best to break through the living room windows. The layer of ore processing soot from the ever-present plume of arsenic and lead that billowed from the smelter stack was doing its best to foul the glass. Rubbing my eyes, I slowly awakened to another weekend in the apartment. The mythology book was on my chest and Miles Davis was still spinning. Down below on the street the bustle of Tacoma was awash in movement. City buses zoomed by on their routes while car horns honked at stop lights with pedestrians waiting for them to change.

To the north, a tugboat on the Foss Waterway moved an empty barge into position at a wharf along Dock Street. In the distance, the stink of crude oil billowed from the refinery, trailing out over the polluted industrial city, overshadowing the once illustrious, and natural beauty of Commencement Bay and Puget Sound.

In the bathroom, I splashed some cold water on my face, then looked in the mirror. Black stubble, and sleepy brown eyes. *I could use a haircut but I'll hold off for now since I'll be with a bunch long-hairs next weekend. Might help me fit in. But man, my skin is so white. Well, that's what you get for living on the rainy side of the state.* Then my stomach started growling.

A plate of scrambled eggs and some hot coffee was the only thing on my mind as I turned on the TV. On KING-5 the *Jetsons* were flying through space, George and Jane and *click.* I changed the channel to KIRO-7 where *Gumby* and *Pokey* were off on an adventure. *Geez, this thing is still on Saturday mornings.* I watched for a minute as the two clay characters were delivering the mail in an old-time western, getting trapped by a rock slide, and *click,* then tried KOMO-4 where *Casper* was on. For some unexplained reason I turned it back to *Gumby* while I cooked something to eat.

After breakfast I dug out my old plaid suitcase from the closet, found the hiking boots, canteen, raincoat, thinking they would be good to take. A carton of Winstons, a brown leather-bound reporter's notebook, all the legal pads I had and ample ballpoint pens. I packed an extra pair of blue jeans, a few T-shirts, sweatshirt, and my black Converse sneakers.

Oh, and my rucksack, where did I leave that?

VI

Helix

The weathered gray concrete structure had a number of store front tenants over the years until a gaggle of young energetic rebels took it over. When that happened the low in stature building came alive with new stories from the underground, the frontwindows now plastered with psychedelic rock concert posters, benefits, events, and artwork. The *Helix* was the headquarters for the counterculture in Seattle. It was within these walls where their crusade combated the draft, Vietnam, and racism, while promoting free love lifestyles, rock music, jazz, protests, and soft drug use.

A white Volvo came to a halt in front of the building. A man dressed in blue jeans and brown corduroy sport coat with a black collar shirt got out of the car and rushed into the building, like he was on a mission. Openly eager for the sunny Friday while holding a smattering of papers in one hand, the man walked through the door grinning wide.

"Sorry I'm late. I had a dentist appointment. How's the next issue coming along?" he said to the room, his upbeat tone was always a delight to the group. A half dozen staff members turned their heads.

"Good morning, Paul," Scott said from the paste-up table.

"We're getting there," John replied, glancing up from reloading his camera. Sharma was over at her desk and smiled when she looked up from the selectric composer, her elfish grin was always addicting.

"Did we get any more firm commitments from bands?"

"Yes," Roxie offered, "The Youngbloods are coming for sure and Country Joe. But still no word from Buffy Sainte-Marie."

"Jauggernaut and Easy Chair will be there," Tim said, setting down his coffee cup. He stroked his dark-moustache and added, “Kalidescope and Phoenix committed. Oh, and The New Lost City Ramblers.”

“Okay, so let’s put together a list of all the confirmed acts. And what about festival ads? Did we get more out?”

“We did,” Walt replied, fidgeting with his glasses. “I’ve got another in the Tacoma News Tribune, one in the Times and another in Seattle Magazine. I ran one in the pictorial last week.”

“Excellent! And what about on the radio?” Paul asked, setting the papers on his desk then taking off his coat, placing it over the back of his chair. He picked up his favorite cup and headed for the coffee machine.

“Oh, yeah. We got that covered,” Roxie said as she typed. Not looking up, she added, “KRAB, KOL, KJR, and even KRKO up in Everett is gonna be running ads all this weekend and next week.”

“Oh,” Scott blurted, “the Camlin Hotel called back finally, they’ve reserved a dozen rooms for each night for us to rotate all the out of town band members through.”

"Great! You guys are the best," Paul replied, sipping his coffee, "but how are we going to pay for all this?"

"Funny you should ask," Walt replied with a grin. "Because Capitol Records just bought a full page for Steve Miller's *Children of the Future*. Columbia bought a page for Mike Bloomfield and Steve Stills' *Super Sessions*, and with a musical big bang for the buck RCA bought two full pages for Jefferson Airplane!"

"Nice! Those will pay the bills this month."

"But after next weekend I want to follow up on those two Panthers getting arrested," Walt added, "Dixon and Harris. Over that so-called stolen typewriter and tie it in with the mass arrest two days later," he said, his young face glowing with earnest intentions. Paul nodded at him.

With his always positive outlook and generous smile, he said, "Go for it. Take the story wherever it takes you."

"I've got some awesome photos of the Panther headquarters you can use for it," John interjected. He touched his denin shirt pocket, grinned, then fiddled some more with his camera.

“Good!”

“Squee-Gee Graphics brought over a far-out map for the festival,” Sharma added. “Good thing we asked Roger to do one because the State Fair is Labor Day weekend too, so US 2 will be packed. It has directions from here through Woodinville to Monroe with the backroads way out to Sultan and Betty’s place.”

“Oh, man,” Paul exclaimed with glee, “next weekend is gonna be a blast. All our work and effort is gonna pay off!”

“No kidding, two months of solid go, go, go,” Tim said.

“Yep, it’s finally happening,” Walt proclaimed.

“Sometimes I can’t believe that we actually pulled it off.”

“Okay, well, we haven’t quite pulled it off yet.”

“But we will. And John and Cyrus will too. We’re all gonna make it happen for sure. We shall prevail.”

"Man, I am so jazzed about Sky River!" John said, standing up from his desk. He glanced over at Tim then headed for the rear door, walking past stacks of old *Helix* issues and paper-filled boxes. Tim and Sharma followed him into the overgrown and hidden backyard.

John fished a crumpled pack of Chesterfields out from his shirt pocket, took one, then held them out for his friends, saying, "Chilly out."

"Fall's in the air, you can feel it," Sharma replied. Once each of them had a cigarette, Tim lit a match and they all enjoyed their morning smoke break.

"Are you still staying at the Dutch Cup next weekend?"

"You bet we are!" Sharma exclaimed. "Roxie and I are gonna live it up. How about you? Are you still thinking you're gonna camp at Bettys?"

"It's all I can affford," John answered as he exhaled his drag of white savory smoke. Then he looked at Sharma and asked, "How much is it?"

"It's like six bucks a night so if you two decide against camping and bunk with us it'll only be a buck and a quarter a night. That's cheap man! And better than sleeping in the dirt the whole time."

"I dunno. Maybe," John replied, stroking his chin. "You know, if the weather turns bad and it rains I don't have a tent."

"For for the love of — you don't wanna get stuck in the rain."

"Well shit, then I'm in for a buck and a quarter a night!"

He looked at Tim. "Yep, I'm in, too."

The reardoor cracked open and Paul stuck his head out, "Is break time over yet? Because we've got work to do."

"Yeah, yeah," Sharma replied. "We're finalizing plans."

"Okay, but hurry it up. We've still got to get over to Lynnwood today to get this issue to the printer and I've got a meeting downtown tonight. So, *andale compadres*!"

"You got it, Helios!" John said, chuckling. "Oh great Son of the Sun who radiates white light upon us and makes this newspaper grind out the ethos that this town needs."

Paul added, "Okay, Apollo," grinning, closing the door.

"I need to come up with a new idea for the *Omega-84* comic strip," Tim said, taking another drag. After he it blew out he exclaimed, "Oh wow! I just had a great thought. Maybe I could work old man Braman into *Omega,* somehow. That would be so funny. But probably piss him off though." he looked at John and grinned.

"That would most definitely piss him off to no end."

"Good! Maybe his head would explode. I'd love to see that" . . . "Ooh! Ooh!" John coughed, "you could put that in it."

They laughed while Sharma blew a smoke ring. She looked at John and said, "Thanks for the ciggy, because, man, oh man, there is nothing better than our breaks on a sunny morning."

VII

The Dog House

John Chambless sat in the back at their occasional table in the diner nursing a Rainier and going over band contracts while he waited for his cohorts to show up. Like every Friday, Dick was seated at the Wurlitzer, his notes of an Irish ballad wafting through the haze of cigarette smoke and the smell of fries in the air.

"Okay, what'll it be, honey," a voice asked, she caught him off guard. John looked up and smiled, seeing the waitress holding her order pad, wearing a white apron, hair in a beehive. She stood expressionless, pencil at the ready.

"Thanks, Marge, but I think I'll wait for the others."

Over her shoulder he saw Paul and Tom come through the door. They strolled past Dick at the organ and nodded, then walked by the old wall photo of the Doberman Pincher, the padded plastic booths, and all the regulars at the bar swilling cocktails and draft beer.

“Oh, here they come now, good, I’m starving.”

Marge turned around as the two pulled out chairs and sat down at the table, both of them grinning like schoolboys.

“What’s it gonna be?” she asked, tapping her foot in wait.

“A Mutt Burger for me, and an Oly, please,” Paul replied. She looked at Tom. “And for you, handsome?”

“Oh, I think I’m gonna have The Pooch, with a bottle of Lucky,” he answered, stroking his mustache. Then he took his rumpled felt cowboy hat off and carefully set it on the empty chair next to himself.

“And you, hon’? What’ll it be tonight?”

“I haven’t had a thing all day, so I’ll go with the liver and onions,” John said, with an eager grin, “and a side of fries.”

"Very good you three, if I might ask, what's with all the papers?"

"Oh, we're putting on a rock festival," John answered.

"A rock festival? You mean like rock-n-roll music?"

"It'll be something that's never been done before," Paul offered.

"Yep, we're going to put lightning in a bottle and send the straight world a message, a real big one," Tom said. Marge gave him a questioning look so Paul added.

"It's going to be an explosion of consciousness!" He spread his arms out over the table as he did. Marge shook her head, turned around, and walked off to the kitchen.

"How you been?" John asked, giving Tom a whimsical look. "You here for the weekend? How's the Apex?"

"Yep, just call me, Picasso Triggerfish! I'm just trying to get along while living on the edge of society unobtrusively, and still doing reviews. Staying up the street working on my story and at the paper on Saturdays. But I am definitely going to be up at Sultan next Sunday."

Grinning, John glanced over at Paul, "As for me, I've been working on the festival every day. I brought a list of all the confirmed acts that we have so far," he said, setting two pieces of paper on the table in front of him.

"And you? How've you been, John? Busy?" Tom asked.

"Well, the temporal aspects of life are what drive me these days, and this rock festival of course. Hell, I could be hit by a train tomorrow and it would be all over. So, let's get this little bit of rock and roll stew cooking."

"How come we're not meeting at the Blue Moon?"

"I thought this would be a nice change of pace," John answered. "And I figured you'd be at the Apex so it's close for you. But really, sometimes there's just too many weirdos at that place, too many hanger's-on."

It was silent for a moment, John and Paul looked at Tom. He sat across from his friends with a mischievous grin, a twinkle in his eye, the look of enlightenment on his face. He twisted in his seat and said, “Sometimes I have these funny out of nowhere thoughts.”

“Yes,” Paul said warmly, “we’ve noticed time to time.”

“Did you know that Monarch butterflies view the world through a retina similar to humans? And that they’re capable of distinguishing colors through their wavelength. They have true color vision, which is so important to everything in their lives. Like how they choose a mate, seeking nectar to nourish themselves, and finding a nesting place. And, get this, they remember certain colors and have learned through evolution that color recognition is vital in their survival — I think that’s so incredibly fascinating.”

“That is wild man,” Paul said, shaking his head.

“Okay, Tom. That’s good stuff,” John said. “But we’ve got to get down to business. I think our main goal is going to be realized. We’ve got a diverse group of performers, not just musicians and bands, but we’ve signed up a comedian, and a mime troupe, too. We’ll have blues, old timey folk, rock, acoustic songwriters, and jazz in the evenings. I'm, we're, going to start each day at 9:30 and then have twelve to eighteen solid hours of music both Saturday and Sunday, but then try to end relatively early on Monday around 6:00 or 7:00. If there are still musicians around who want to jam after the last act then I think we should let them."

"Holy moly, John. That's a ton of music and acts," Tom remarked.

"I know, but between Paul and his staff at the *Helix* we are going to make it work. It'll be a solid weekend of eclectic artists and culture that will set the tone for years to come."

"Everyone on the staff is working their butts off," Paul remarked.

"Yes, thank you for that. We're doing something that's never been done before and taking in the whole spectrum while we do it. You know, bring everything together in a colorful display where the arts meet counterculture. All of it in one place, at the same time. There's going to be as many genres as we can have in an explosion of sight and sound."

"And how are the ticket sales so far."

“We’ve sold about nine-thousand and counting.”

“Nine-thousand? No kidding,” Paul replied. “There’s gonna be a lot of traffic out there.”

“Cyrus and I’ve got that handled. We swung a deal with the local berry farmers to use their buses to shuttle festival goers from their fields out to the site. We’re letting them charge for parking in exchange for their busses. However, we have a problem. We are close to being over budget.”

“Crap, really?”

“Yes, because to get good quality music, the kind that our audience will want, we are paying union scale. It’s two-hundred and fifty dollars for Santana, and I’ve never heard their music before. I mean, I’ve heard of them, and gotten good reports, but they don’t have a record out. Then there’s everything else — we are paying for all the bands airplane flights, who don’t live in the area, and then shuttle them to the site and pay for their overnight accommodations at the Camlin Hotel. We are chartering a bus to take musicians to and from the Camlin and Sea-Tac and to the venue, but in a pinch, I’ve got Pete Freemont with his Econoline van and

Mike Carmichael and his station wagon who've volunteered to shuttle in case we need them. We've got SaniKan's that we are paying for, ticket printing, catering, a huge generator, stage construction, and the art collective is doing twelve-foot-high painted plywood walls that will jut fifty-feet out from both sides of the stage. They'll be built kind of like an accordion, you know, like a zig zag thing that will provide some color and be a barrier between the audience and the backstage area. Plus, we have to rent a PA and pay two soundmen. We've got a parking location in Sultan, one in Monroe, and a land owner has come forward that's really close to the site. I've worked a deal with him so he can charge for car and bus camping. So, it's all been pretty overwhelming at times."

"Yeah, well. It's worth it," Tom replied, grinning, then added, "because God's own rhythm section is going to bring it all home next weekend at Betty Nelson's Organic Raspberry Farm."

VIII

Sultan

Chunks of bark and sprigs of Evergreen needles dotted the highway, a log scaling station, and then traffic slowed. I did a double take seeing two converted school buses parked at Gene's Chevron. *It looks like small town America is getting a wake-up call.* It announced the hippie presence and was apparent that the rebel youth had arrived. One bus was painted military green; it had a large load of long poles fastened to its roof. *What are those for?* The other was covered with brightly colored dayglo painted strokes, except for the words **Flower Power** in pink. The rest of its exterior was swirling shapes, and abstract lines with no discernable objective or outcome. It was Jackson Pollock on wheels.

A gaggle of long-haired kids were walking along the main highway drag. The farther I got into town there were even more of them, everywhere. Sultan had been invaded by itinerant hipsters, it was overflowing. Laden with heavy backpacks, wearing dirty blue jeans or cut-offs, they all looked like they were from another planet. I'd never seen so many hippies in one place in my life. Groups sat on the ground in circles, some playing acoustic guitars, other's throwing frisbees along the railroad tracks. Two girls with long blonde hair were holding hands and skipping down the side of the road without a care in the world, oblivious to everything.

At the main intersection an overweight state patrol and a sad-faced deputy were directing traffic, blowing whistles and gesturing at me to hurry up and drive on through. The exasperation on their faces told the world that they wished they were anywhere else. Up ahead a pick-up load of what appeared to be local high school kids was coming the opposite way, all of them gawking at the hippie horde that had descended upon their peaceful little place, including the driver, who distracted, had crossed the white line. I had no choice but to hit my horn and luckily, he swerved away.

As I pulled in to the Dutch Cup parking lot I noticed a tall lanky fellow walking away from it with an odd kind of gait. Bermuda shorts, a preppie shirt, visor on his head, and tennis shoes with no socks. He clutched a long cigarette holder in his teeth. *I wonder if he's staying here?* The parking lot was nearly full and a few long-haired couples were about, but their clothes were clean so I guessed they were high-class hippies, if there was such a thing. I parked the Impala, got my suitcase out from the back seat and headed for the office with my paid receipt already in my shirt pocket.

There was a new person behind the counter, a fellow with black framed glasses in a white pressed shirt and clean shaven. He stood expressionless as he watched me walk in not saying a word, without a greeting.

"Good evening. I'm Cliff McCalister and I've got room number 25 reserved."

Still saying nothing, he ran his finger down the ledger until he stopped and then lowered his head closer to read the reservation. "Yes, we've got you paid for four nights."

"Good, I just drove all the way up from Tacoma. Long way."

"You're here for the rock festival, I take it?"

"I'm from the News Tribune, got stuck with it."

"You and me both," he replied, handing over the key.

"Enjoy your stay. Oh, and the restaurant closes at 8:00."

In the room, I dropped the heavy suitcase on the bed. Opening it, I tossed the yellow legal pads on the small desk at the window and set two pens next to them. Then put my reporter's notebook and a pen in my back pocket, the Winstons in my shirt, and checked for some matches. I decided to walk back into the main part of town.

At Fifth Street I looked up and down the way. Hippie kids were everywhere and I wanted to talk to some of them but was hungry. Up the street was the Loggers Inn and, on the highway's corner, sat the Pass Time Tavern, The Sportsman's Café on the opposite. The Pass Time had a good ring to it so I walked in the door.

The place was choked with smoke and country music played. *Someone's taking someone else back home and making old memories come alive at the same time.* Everything went quiet, except the jukebox. Heads turned as I came in, but when they saw I wasn't a long-hair, they all went back to their beers and conversations.

Hard-faced men in white T-shirts or flannel mackinaw, wearing chainsaw hats and suspenders sat in groups, some with their wives, all with long faces. It was easy to see that they were concerned with their town's situation. These folks were the salt and spirit of the community. Toiling in the woods or farms, the schools and churches, most with dirt under their fingernails. And here I was, searching to understand the fate by which they'd found themselves. Them, trying like me, to understand the free spirits who had crashed into their lives, all of them landing like a dirty heap of laundry at their doorstep — them — the unwashed and unwanted.

The fellow I'd seen earlier in the Bermuda shorts was at the bar talking with what appeared to be a local man, he was the only one wearing sunglasses. His long-stemmed cigarette holder jutted out over the counter, the smoke rising up like a miniature campfire. There was an empty table by a window. I sat down and quickly noticed the menu under the glass top with a cartoon drawing of a Paul Bunyon type of character with oversized boots, an axe, and chainsaw. *Classy place.*

"What'll it be," a woman's voice asked. I looked up and saw a waitress in an apron, *Doreen* on her name tag. She stood over me chewing gum, smacking away with her pad and pen at the ready. One look at her teased-out mess of hair told me exactly how much time she'd wasted doing so, it was a beehive of kinky dishwater blonde cotton candy.

"Oh, hi, I guess, um, I'll try the Basin Burger, no mayo."

"And to drink?"

"Have you got any cold Heidelberg? In a bottle?"

"We sure do Hun, anything else? A side of onion rings?"

"Oh, no, that's alright, but it comes with fries, right?"

"We've got the best fries in town, Sugar" she said, turning away. Seconds later she came back with my beer and a plastic bowl of pretzels. I smiled at her then tried one after she left. *Oh my god . . . these things are old.*

Looking around, I remembered a few faces from the town hall meeting the week before when the mayor walked in. Searching my mind for his name, by the time it dawned on me, he'd already taken a seat with a woman. She was the best-looking gal in the place, his wife no doubt. So, I went back to people watching. At a table near me sat four men, two empty pitchers, full ashtrays, and a whole bunch of worry.

"Jesus, the heck," complained one of them with a gray beard, "these damn kids are gonna burn down all our houses and steal our women! Not to mention every hubcap in town. For the love of Christ, what're we supposed to do? Load our guns and sit at home by the window and wait for them to loot and raise hell?"

"Damn it, Virgil, they're just kids. They ain't criminals."

"Yeah, well, not yet," he replied, burping. "But I'm keepin' my doors locked all weekend. Mary Jane is worried sick, Grandma too. It's gonna be anarchy here for the next three days. I don't like it one bit."

"Anarchy? Really, Virgil? Not gonna happen. Not so."

"I heard they take that LDS stuff every day, dropped outta school every one of 'em. Just worthless punks."

"It ain't LDS, it's called LSD or acid with other fancy colorful names. I read all about it in Time magazine."

Outside, the highway was backed up, long-hairs, kids, and VW vans were everywhere. It was a hippie pilgrimage, all of them headed to the promised land. The town was so full I was sure that they'd never ever seen anything like this before. I reached behind and pulled my notebook and pen out their hiding place and started jotting down some notes. The words came slow at first, but then the wildly colored dayglo bus turned and went across the bridge that headed south, towards where most of the kids were going. I knew where they were off to and was just barely beginning to get a small sense for the situation, a sense for my story, where to start and what to put down.

The small rural town of Sultan, site of the Sky River Rock Festival, was overwhelmed with hippie youth here for a 3-day music festival. The highway and side roads became a cluttered mass of converted school buses, VW vans, hitchhikers, and groups of hippies who all descended upon this traditional logging town. A parade of adventurous youth, hundreds of gypsy-like travelers on a spiritual quest, searching for the magic of the moment in music and community, looking for a new experience and new beginning, existing in a live and let live life and all of them looking for a new model of reality, hoping to find truth on the byways of the cosmic frontier.

Wow, what just happened? I knew of and had read those words before but I'd never used them or written like that —

"Here you go, sweetie," Doreen said, setting down an overflowing plate of French fries with a burger.

"Thanks."

Glancing around after being lost in thought, I noticed the Bermuda shorts guy had left but the fellows near me were still carrying on about all the invaders.

Looking out the window at the kids walking on the south bridge, the same logger motioned with flip of his hand and remarked. "There they go, heading out to Betty's to have their little shin-dig clam bake thing and it doesn't even start until tomorrow . . . and of course those Seattle people putting it on just had to find the one and only hippie in the valley. Hell, my boy Jake and his cousin Adam are planning on kicking some hippie butt this weekend," he said, with a grin like a mean badger. "I even paid for their tickets. Those worthless, no school, no work bums are gonna get with they deserve. They'll never see what's coming."

"For Christ sakes, Virgil. What the hell are you talking about? They're just kids that like music, leave 'em be. They're no threat to you, your son, or his cousin. Give it up."

"Them hippies are a threat to society, and this country. Hell, our boys are over fightin' in Vietnam and these bums are just a bunch of draft dodgers!"

"Virgil, stop it. Don't be givin' our town a black eye. And you don't know they're dodging the draft. Most of them are college kids on summer break — and you're not gonna make the world a better place by having them beat up a bunch of harmless hippies. So don't you dare turn this weekend into some kind of riot."

"Those punks need to learn the lessons they ain't never learned," Virgil stated defiantly with a scowl.

"Virgil, you're drunk, go home and sleep it off."

☼

After finishing my meal I noticed that the mayor was still seated at his table, albeit with friends now. It was an opportunity that I couldn't let slip away so I got up with pen and notebook in hand and walked over to him.

"Mr. Mayor, sir," I offered, sticking out my hand. "I met you last week at the town hall meeting, Cliff McCalister."

"Oh yes," he replied, looking up, "I remember you." He shook my hand but stayed seated, then crossed his arms.

"Could I get a quote for my Tacoma readers about what's going on right now, you know, with the hippies and such?"

He paused for a moment to gather his thoughts, then said, "So far, it's been good. I did get a call from Mrs. Gunderson though, with a complaint about some kids walking down her alley smoking something suspicious. But overall things have been generally quiet."

"Okay, so, obviously the efforts to stop the festival failed."

"Yes, they did, and actually as long as there are no problems the city council and myself included will be happy."

"Are you planning on attending it? Did you buy tickets?"

"Gosh no. I'll be at my office manning the phones all weekend."

"The job of being mayor never stops, does it?"

"Yep. That's right. It's kinda like show business, I guess."

"Meaning?"

"Well, it's apparent to me that the show must go on."

Just then three long-hairs walked in the door and the whole place went silent. Virgil leapt to his feet pointing with a menacing look on his face and blurted loudly, "You damn hippies! Get the hell outta here! Now!"

Heads turned back and forth from Virgil to the long-hairs and back to him. With shocked looks on their faces the three walked backwards and out the door as most in the tavern cheered.

"Would you like to comment on what we just saw, Mr. Mayor?" I asked, taking notes.

"Nope."

"Any other comments you'd like to make at this time?"

The mayor grinned then looked out the window at the people and cars headed across the south bridge and said, "I will offer a word of advice though, keep your car in town tomorrow and use the parking lot here, ride their bus. The lot is just a few blocks back on the highway at Reese's berry farm," he said, gesturing west.

"Right, I think I saw the parking sign on the way into town. Thanks for the advice. I appreciate that."

Outside the sun was setting but hordes of kids were still showing up. Hitchhikers most of them. I saw a group jumping out of the bed of a pick-up truck.

"Hey, you hippies!" I hollered, and started walking towards them. "Can I ask you a few questions?"

Three guys and one girl, teenagers, all of them carrying overflowing sherpa sized back packs stuffed with food and sleeping bags. As I got closer, I detected some sort of perfume, sweet and earthy. All of them dressed in what I was learning to be the standard uniform; beaded chokers and necklaces, leather and silver bracelets, denim jackets, boots or tennis shoes, rings, and lots of hair. The girl was carrying a transistor radio in her hand blasting at peak volume, the deejay talking over the guitar intro.

Heavy guitar riff at the beginning then the singer came on about how the sun was coming up and that he'd soon be with someone in the morning dawn with the sunshine, Falling stars and how long he's been waiting. Lots of loud guitar solos and banging of drums.

One had a folded-up canvas tarp tied to the side of his pack and another held a plastic milk jug half-filled with water, he looked the oldest and had an honest face, but a quick dispossession.

“We’re not hippies’ man,” he barked, “we’re Heads!”

“Oh, sorry. So, um, where’re you Heads coming from?”

“Portland.”

“Wow, no kidding. You hitchhiked the whole way from Oregon?”

“You bet, it took all day. We hit the road at 7:00 and sure enough, we made it to the promised land. This weekend we are gonna get back to the country!”

“Our first ride got us all the way to Olympia, and then Seattle and Everett, and now we’re here. It’s so far out, man,” the fellow with the tarp replied, eyes bloodshot.

“That’s right, dude. We are gonna be groovin’ all weekend!”

I turned to the girl; buxom, long blonde hair with a red headband, no make-up, faded and patched blue jeans, a white peasant blouse, and braless. She had an angelic face, was a capturing presence, and I lost my train of thought momentarily.

"Are you all a traveling family? Brothers and sisters?"

"You could say that, I guess," she replied with an engaging smile. "We're all high school friends. Bobby graduated last year but the rest of us will be seniors."

"Okay, I see . . . and, what about your parents? Do they know that you're all the way up here in Sultan?"

"Sure do," the girl answered. "My folks are cool."

"Yeah, man. My Mom paid for my ticket and gave me five bucks. She's the absolute best!"

"She did?" the older one snapped, "you didn't tell us that!"

"Sorry. It's just that, she gives me money all the time."

"What's with all the questions, man. Who are you?"

"Oh, sorry. I'm with the Tacoma News Tribune.

I'm Cliff McCalister on assignment to get the real skinny." *Geez, shoot me now, I just sounded like my boss.*

"Shit man . . . he's an investigative reporter. Here to investigate us."

"No, no. I'm not. I'm just a run of the mill reporter here to do an in-depth feature article on the rock festival."

"Aw, bull-shit. You're an investigator — oh man — that's so establishment. No more news flash for you." They all turned and walked away.

By the time I got back to the motel parking lot it was dusk and a very distinct dank smell hit my nose. Just as I came round the corner, I caught a glimpse of two well-dressed hipster chicks ducking from the upper balcony and into their room. *Hmm, were they smoking cigarettes? But that didn't smell like cigarettes to me. Hey! That was pot! There's gonna be a lot of that this weekend.*

Right when I slipped my key into the lock, I heard the sound of an electric typewriter coming from the room next to me. It stopped, then a wild screech sounded, "Eeooww!" Like some ancient warrior coming down from the hills to rape and pillage an enemy village.

What in the hell was that? The typing started again. A stop, start, jumpy kind of rhythm to it. The ding of the bell as the carriage hit the return seemed to slam like a metal cudgel, banging through the wall. On and on it went when his phone rang. The conversation started with muffled talk but then it escalated to what sounded like a disagreement which shifted to all out verbal warfare. *Was he getting a divorce? Bad news from the home front?* Next, the slamming down of the phone and his door opened quickly. I peeked through the blinds. It was the Bermuda shorts guy, heading to the ice machine with an empty bucket, barefooted and shirtless, his cigarette holder leading him forward.

IX

Day One

After a night of dreamless sleep, screeching, howling, phone calls, and typewriter banging next door, it was a joy to wake up to quiet. I laid on the bed and closed my eyes again, enjoying the peace and solitude, thinking I could get a few more moments of shut-eye. But then I sat straight up and looked at my watch. *Holy crap it's almost eight o'clock!*

I took a quick shower, got dressed, grabbed my rucksack and keys and made my way to the café, for a good old country breakfast. Inside, the first thing I saw was the Bermuda shorts guy. He had a table of what looked like half the menu in front of him, and nearly eaten already. Two glasses of grapefruit juice, one empty, coffee, a bowl of fruit, pancakes, cereal, a Bloody Mary, omlette, a pile of napkins and an ashtray. He had a copy of the Seattle P-I open that he was reading and muttering about the headlines.

Unbelievable! Who on earth is this guy and why is he here?

“Morning,” I offered. He looked up, took the cigarette holder out of his mouth, adjusted his sunglasses, and said, “Good Mornin’.”

I sat down at the empty table across from him wondering how to engage. He was obviously excentric but, I couldn’t quite put my finger on what it was about him, he seemed like someone I should try to get to know. I guessed he was here for the rock show; however, he didn’t look or act like any kind of hip music critic.

I couldn’t help myself. “Are you here for the rock festival?”

In between bites he set the paper down and looked over at me, grinned, then said, “I am. And you?”

“Me too. Cliff McCalister. Tacoma News Tribune.”

“Well, Cliff McCalister,” he replied smiling, he folded the newspaper in half and set it aside, saying, “good to meet you.”

He went back to his enormous meal, taking a bite of pancake then bringing the Bloody Mary up to his lips. He took a long sip then made a cough-like gurgling sound.

"And — you are?" I asked in the best, politest tone I could.

He glanced over to me and cleared his throat. I didn't think he was going to answer but then he said, "I'm Hunt . . . Raoul Duke, here to take a look at things. Maybe get a handle on what's happening way up here in rural America. You know, pick at the real meat and bones."

"So, you're a reporter, too. I thought you might be —"

"What'll it be Sweetie?" a familiar voice asked. It was Doreen from the night before. *Boy is this a small town.* I didn't even look at the menu.

"How about biscuits and gravy. Can I get that and a coffee?"

"You bet Sugar," she said, then asked, "You want cream?" I nodded, 'yes.' After she left, without turning my head, I looked from the corner of my eye back at Raoul. He was scarfing his meal, downing everything on the table. He was done in no time, as he got up to go, he slapped some cash on the table, then looked at me with an earnest grin and said, "Okay. Good to meet you. I'll see you at the big dance." He turned to go but stopped, "Oh, and remember. Breakfast's the most important meal of the day." As I watched him leave, I knew there was something about him but I just couldn't put my finger —

"Here you go Sweetie. Can I get you anything else?"

"Oh, yes. Could I get a turkey sandwich to go? No mayo."

I took the mayor's advice and found the parking lot in town, a fleet of school buses and one charter. From outward appearances the motorcoach looked like a repurposed '50s Greyhound, like a grand dame as it sat idling, an awaiting carriage. But once I stepped on board the malodor of stale cigarettes and cleaning agent fought hard to take her glory days of high travel away.

"Morning," I said to the potbellied gray headed driver.

"Same to you," he replied, smiling with confidence. He looked like he was physically part of the bus, wedged into his seat, the years of service he'd waged clearly visible by the wrinkles on his face. I could tell that he was in charge, at the controls and still proud to be captain of his once mighty and celebrated ship.

"You're lucky. This is my only festival run today. Gotta go to Sea-Tac after this for a pick up and drive back."

I found a comfy but sagging soft brown seat and set my backpack down. The coach's notable old charm was comforting, however, there were only a dozen other riders on board. *Where is everybody? How come we're not full?*

Just as the driver grabbed the chrome handle to lever the door closed, a dented and scratched up Chevy Apache pick-up barreled into the lot. *That's the same truck that nearly ran me off the road yesterday.* In the bed were four teenage boys, two in the cab, most of them with crew-cuts and white T-shirts, a few had packs of smokes rolled up in their left-side short sleeve. Once parked all of them ran over, hopped on board and went to take seats in the very back, snickering.

9:28 am

Riding out to the festival the sky was overcast but the weather looked promising. Out on the highway we turned right to head across the river to the site, the rolling hulk of heavy metal creaking and swaying. The bridge bended upward in a graceful arch, crystal-clear water in the Skykomish River below. To the east, the jagged peaks of the Cascades rose upward in a majestic statement. Once on the other side and away from the bustle of the highway and town, it was a different world. Lush green pastures between shallow sloughs and cattail wetlands, overgrown forests carpeted by sword ferns and the meandering Skykomish, bold and beautiful since the ancients had plied its water. Just then my heart skipped a beat, and an inner jolt of voltage buzzed up my spine. *What was that*? My body tingled with energy. Was it because I was out in the county, close to the wilderness and the motherland, traveling forward, moving towards an unseen and unknown destination? For some unexplained reason it sure felt good.

There were a few Heads along the way, one with a piece of cardboard with 'I need a free ticket' written on it. We made a turn past a small farm house then continued up and over short hills and towering trees that formed a multi-layered overhead canopy. One country home had a mud-splattered logging truck parked in its yard where a man stood with his hands on his hips and a scowl on his face as we went by. The teenagers in back seemed agitated, hitting their fists in open palms and pointing at some hippies along the way. They opened a window as we got close to another long-haired group, one stuck his head out of the window and yelled, “We'll see you soon, ya' stupid hippies!”

“Nice one, Jake,” his buddy said, slapping him on the back. My ears perked up hearing that name from the night before.

“Okay folks,” the driver said over the intercom, stepping on his air brakes as we eased to a halt. “Here we are.” When he pulled the lever to open the door he added, “I can go up to the Cedar Ponds campsite next, if anyone needs to go there, it's less than a mile away.”

Out the windows I saw cars lined along the county road and people walking. A gravel road across from us went up a slight grade and next to it sat a kiosk built out of 2 x 4s with a metal roof. A few people were milling about, Jake and his boon companions hopped off the bus then ran to the ticket stand just as a light blue Ford station wagon pulled up and stopped. Two grinning teenage girls hopped out while a wide-eyed kid in a boy scout uniform watched from a backseat window. As I stepped off, rock music, banging drums, loud guitars and vocals filled the air. Then a '58 beat-up black Plymouth Belvedere four-door sedan, gashed and dented with Oregon plates, came to a halt in a cloud of black engine smoke. Three heads got out with their gear, the car barreled off to find a parking place, running rough, burning oil.

"If you don't have a weekend ticket then day tickets are four bucks. Step right up, step right up," the ticket taker crowed like a carnival barker. He had a long beard, wore oval rose-colored glasses and a top hat with red and black stripes. I went and stood behind the Oregon guys.

They looked prepared for the duration. Laden with over-stuffed backpacks, sleeping bags, tarps, two of them shirtless, one had a peace sign medallion hanging from his neck, faded jeans and hiking boots. "Oh man," he said quietly, "six bucks for the weekend. Shit, I don't have any more money, none." He turned to his buddy and whispered, “What am I gonna do now?”

“No worries, how about we take ourselves a little walk.”

Off they went up the road so I stepped forward to the kiosk. Fastened to the plywood sides were colorful posters, one read, Sky River Rock Festival & Lighter Than Air Fair — All Profits go to Native American Organizations. A large brooding man with thick black hair stood next to the ticket guy, eyeing each person warily as they either paid or had their three-day ticket stub removed. He gave Jake and his buddies the stink eye as they coughed up their passes.

“Afternoon,” I said, holding out my three-day ticket. “I’m here from the News Tribune in Tacoma. I’d like to see if I could speak with some of the organizers, if possible.”

“And you are?” the big guy said, taking a giant step forward.

“Cliff McCalister, here’s my card,” I answered, quickly handing it over, smiling. “I’ll only need a minute of time.”

"Hmm, Cliff McCalister, you say," big fella replied, looking at the card. "You're here from Tacoma?"

"Yes, all weekend. The paper is having me do a feature article."

"A big, positive article, right?" he added, giving me the look over.

"Absolutely."

"Okay, Cliff. You've already paid, and you look legit. I'll take you up and find John for you, he's the music director. Cy's here today, too, but they're both real busy. Since you're here every day I think it'd be best that I introduce you and if they have time, you can talk. But if not then you may have to wait until tomorrow." I nodded in agreement and slung my rucksack over a shoulder with a wide smile.

He started walking up the gentle grade and motioned for me to follow. "Okay, thank you, and your name is?"

"I'm Roger, head of security and friend of the family." *Interesting, head of security and family friend.*

We passed under a banner archway, 'Welcome to The Sky River Rock Festival' in colorful lettering, an Indian headdress painted at each end of it in soft earthy tones. The music was getting louder with every step.

Someone's putting a spell on someone else, But there's a witch and some lying going on.

"So, those kids that were ahead of me, I think they're looking to make some trouble," I offered, trying to get on his good side. "I overheard them on the bus talking about beating up hippies today. I thought you might want to know, seeing how you're handling those things."

He turned to me and said, "Thanks, I appreciate that. I had a feeling about them and we've heard the rumors about a few of the locals not being too happy about us."

With each step up the slight grade the festival came more and more into view and then — I arrived. What spread out before me was like no toga party I'd ever been to. It was a soupy mélange of hundreds of thrill-seekers and freaks in boots, sandals, some barefoot, tye-die and white thrift store blouses, fringe, patched over blue jeans and more hair than anywhere in the world. There was a farmhouse sided with cedar shingles with a covered porch, a barn, pigs in a pen, horses and long strings of raspberry trellises.

A large stage with banks of huge black speakers pointed outward towards a gentle uphill natural amphitheater. Tall plywood walls had been erected outward from each side of the stage showing painted shapes done in pastel hues with lavender, pink and purple; a palette of soft tranquil colors. Thousands of people either sitting on blankets, looking for camping spots or dancing, and what the — a huge hot air balloon began to rise — floating mid-air. I stopped and stared at it. *What on earth?! Unbelievable*! Vertical red, white, and blue stripes with a small chair hanging under it and all tethered by rope and tied to the bumper of a truck. It was surrounded by hippies and forestland while smothered in a hanging particulate of pot smoke that held sway over the encampment. *That stuff sure smells better than cigarettes . . . kinda good.*

A balding, heavy-set fellow was handling ballon rides, I heard him say, “All riders must have the proper attitude before they can achieve any altitude. Got it?”

"Hey!" Roger hollered over the music, "are you coming?"

"Oh, sorry." He led me to the roped off back-stage area where dozens of people were gathered. Most of them musicians standing around with guitars strapped on their shoulders, drum kits sat on the ground in disarray or in the back of vans with their doors open where amplifiers sat waiting. Piles of lumber, paint cans, and plywood were strewn about, a long ramp went up to the stage for hauling equipment. A huge generator whirred behind and below the bank of the hill and power cables were everywhere underfoot. There was a red cross over an entrance to one tent with a sign, Open Door Clinic. At another larger circus-like wall tent with red and white stripes, people were coming and going with beers or plates of food in their hands, smiling, talking, and the music was loud and clear.

There's a woman named Susie Q and a guy liked the way that she walked and how she talked.

My heart started to race, it was exciting to be so close to the music and the people who played it, and the women. Beautiful hip women in long flowing dresses, smoking, flirting, laughing. It was invigorating to be right next to it. I followed Roger over to a group of people where a man was talking to some long-haired fellas who I guessed were the next act. He looked serious, and confident as he spoke to them wearing a black vest over a white collared shirt, pressed blue jeans. His dark hair wasn't long like them, it was combed and he was cleanshaven, looking professional. Just then another man, heavyset with a well-trimmed beard walked up to him, he looked familiar.

The band stopped and ended their set to screams and cheers. "Thank you everyone! Thank you, Sky River!"

"Alright! Buddha here again! Let's give Phoenix a big hand!" he said over the sound system. "Okay, okay, how's everybody doing today?" The crowd roared back in approval. "Good! Good! Sounds like you're all doing fine! So, I want to let you all in on a secret," he said, the crowd quieting. "I guess The Beatles heard about our little get together and they might just show up this weekend."

A few cheers broke out, but then a ripple of skepticism moved through the crowd.

“Alright!”

“Far-out!”

“No way! The Beatles? Not happening!”

“Bullshit, man. The Beatles aren’t coming to Sky River! Yeah, right?”

“Okay, okay. We'll see, we'll see. Next up we've got the Peanut Butter Conspiracy but while they set up, we've got comedian Richard Pryor to entertain us. Both the Peanut Butter Conspiracy and Mister Pryor came up all the way from Los Angles to be here, let’s welcome Richard Pryor, everybody!”

A skinny black man walked out from the side of the stage with a big grin. When he grabbed the microphone his eyes became saucer-like, then he looked out over the crowd, and started laughing.

“Thank you! Haha! Thank you!” Pryor hollered. He walked back and forth as he gazed at everyone, smiling and nodding, then started in. “Can you believe all this talk about nuclear war? Y’all grew up with duck and cover, right?” While Pryor continued with his witticism Roger saw his opening and motioned that it was time to go over and meet the two men who were in the middle of a salubrious conversation. The one in the vest held a clipboard in his hand, flipping pages back and forth.

“Well, it looks like we pulled it off just in time.”

“Yep, so far, so good. What about It’s a Beautiful Day? Did we get a confirmation from them yet?”

“We did. We got a call last night at the house from their manager. They’ll be arriving today and set to play tomorrow or Monday. I’m very happy about that.”

“And what about Big Mama Thornton? Any word there?”

The one fellow looked through his clipboard pages again, found what he needed, then said, “Yes, she’ll be here on Monday for sure. But I still haven’t heard anything from Steppenwolf or Buffy Sainte-Marie.”

“And what about the local *gendarmes*? What’s their take on us so far?”

“I spoke with Deputy Briggs earlier and he assured me that they would keep to the county road and leave us alone, unless that is, there's an injury or serious problem."

"Well, I would hope that they won't consider coming up here for a complaint about loud music."

"Nope. I asked him specifically about that and he said they wouldn't."

"John. Cy," Roger said, approaching the men. "I've got a reporter here that's come up from Tacoma who wanted to see if he could have a moment of time, possibly?"

They stopped at hearing Roger's voice and turned to him. "Yes, Roger, what do you need?" John asked, shoving a hand deep into his blue jeans pocket.

"I just wanted to introduce Cliff McCalister, from the News Tribune in Tacoma." They both glanced at me and nodded, then stuck out their hands. "Cliff, this is John Chambless and Cyrus Noe."

"Good to meet you, Cliff. What can we help you with?" Cyrus said, the look of an eager, busy man on his face.

“I recognize you from the Sultan town hall last week,” I said to him, then shook both their hands. He gave me a quizzical look.

“Oh, you were there were you? That was something.”

“Yes, I remember. So, ah, I know you’re both busy,” I replied. “I’m here all weekend to do a feature article and just wanted to see if I could chat about the festival and how it came about. Things like that,” I said, notebook and pen out.

Another man walked up to us. He glanced at everyone, then said, “I’m sorry to interrupt but the generator is using far more fuel than we anticipated and I just got a report about drug dealers walking around with cardboard signs, like advertisements for dope and LSD. Plus, the clinic has been getting lots of cut feet from broken glass and barbed wire. Smokey says—”

“Okay, Stan, we’ll need to address all that,” Cyrus said to him. “But give us a minute, I’ll deal with those things right away.”

Just then a huge gasp came over the crowd and people started yelling and screaming, Pryor stopped telling his next joke and blurted, “Holy motherfucker! I think somebody needs to call out the Air Force because that balloon looks like it's gonna float away. Son of a —"

John and Cyrus' eyes instantly lit up, they just about bugged right out of their heads, both took off running and I followed. "Where's Jug!" Chambless hollered, running around the stage and back out front. "Where is Van Over?!?" John hollered. "Yeah, where's Larry?" Cyrus added.

Hundreds of people surrounded the truck that the balloon used to be fastened to, most of them looking up towards the sky, pointing and watching the balloon float off. I followed them as they pushed their way through the mass of people standing around, waiting.

"Where is he? Where's Larry? Is there anybody up in that thing? What the hell happened?" The same heavyset man with long hair and receding hairline and thick moustache appeared, looking shocked, out of sorts.

"No, no, there's nobody in it! Thank God! I had it tied down, but," he said, breathing hard, "the rope just gave way. I guess the darn thing worked its way out of the knot I tied and wasn't tight enough, floated off."

"Jesus, Jug," John replied, "who the hell taught you how to tie a knot? Christ! You're just damn lucky there was no one in it." John stopped to get his breath and think for a moment. "Betty doesn't have a phone so you'll need to get yourself down to town and find a pay phone or knock on a neighbor's door and call the FAA right away. Like now!"

"Really?"

"Yes Larry, go and call the Federal Aviation Administration! We need to notify them because of air traffic concerns. Tell them that *you've* got a stray balloon in the sky," he said, looking up as Larry did too, "that it's moving east and, thank goodness, there's not anyone on board. Oh, and don't mention this festival, just tell them you were doing it on your own."

I watched as Larry headed off to make his call then I put my notebook and pen back in the backpack. Roger and Cy disappeared into the crowd and John, who breezed right by me without a word, walked backstage while Mr. Pryor handed the microphone to the MC, Buddha, with a wave and a smile to the crowd.

"Okay! Alright! I guess it's not every day that you get to watch a hot air balloon take off on its own! Next up, all the way from LA, The Peanut Butter Conspiracy!"

10:58 am

I looked for Raoul but didn't see him so I thought a walk around to take in the sights would be a good start. For some unexplained reason I headed straight for the tree line to hike the perimeter instead of going through the maze of blankets and bodies. Like some kind of soldier, automatically seeking higher ground.

Lucious tones wafted through the ether from a wooden flute played by a lady adorned in love beads with feathers in her hair. Bubbles floated softly on a joss stick breeze blown by a goateed man in a brocade jacket with a lace collar. Two smiling girls with small helium ballons tied to their floating hair sauntered past. They were followed by a woman with porcelain skin in red patent leather high heels wearing a fur bikini and black velvet cape, her honey-colored hair in a bouffant. She had the look of enchantment on her face and was cause célèbre — glitterati on the red carpet at a movie premier. I saw Lee Remick in her eyes. *Was I witnessing a seamless group search for inspiration, identity, and true liberty? Was this a new unfolding religion or was it a reexamination of past moral values and societal norms being explored in real time*? It felt like everyone was being reborn all at once, a sense of change was afoot. It was as if this bold new group of seekers were actively transforming from a traditionally based upbringing into a new dominion of experienced based consciousness. An endless number of possibilities hung in the air, awaiting discovery.

The smell of pot was pleasing but the scent of the duff and cedar boughs cleared my mind as I stepped past large sword ferns, fireweed, and the velvety foxglove. Looking up, people were climbing trees, others were sitting and hanging out on massive hemlock limbs, passing joints and carrying on without a care in the world. Halfway to the top of the slope I heard the sounds of joyful groaning, then a yelp of extasy. Glancing into the woods of tall ferns and moss-covered forest floor I saw a sleeping bag going up and down between all the foliage. I couldn't help but stop and stare at it for a few seconds.

"Can you believe that Creedence Clearwater just played?" a man's voice said. I turned and saw a wild-eyed hippie before me. He looked like an alley cat, swarthy, thick dark eyebrows, scruffy beard, a fuzzy fop of hair, and dilated eyes. I had no idea where he came from, he just magically appeared.

“Creedence?”

“It’s unbelievable, right? They were so awesome. I love them!”

I’d just heard the MC say they were Phoenix so I wasn’t sure what to make of his claim when it hit me. He’s wacked-out on pot or maybe LSD.

“So, um, I think that band was called Phoenix and they were playing some Creedence songs.”

“Aw, man,” he replied with a tight jaw. “I know it was Creedence!”

As he left, he moved his hanging arms in unison, skipping back down below to his festival friends.

“Andy! Hey Andy! Wait up!” a woman’s voice cried out. A skinny long-haired lady came bounding out of the trees, waving. She was wild-eyed and free as the wind, too. It was good to see that they were companions, fellow travelers to be with, and watch over each other, hopefully.

Onward and upward I went and soon came upon a shirtless man in cutoffs sitting with his legs crossed, meditating. In his lap was a cardboard sign that read, Orange Sunshine $1. His eyes were glazed over and transfixed in a stare down with the cosmos. The hair on his arms was standing on end and a golden aura radiated outward from his body. I quietly slipped by him.

At the top was a moss-covered log resting on the forest floor surrounded by alder trees. I sat down on it and looked out over the festivities while the Peanut Butter Conspiracy played.

Someone is turning on a friend, Getting your friend stoned, And to not be a miser and instead you'd be much wiser, For having done it.

I dug out the notebook and pen from the backpack then gazed out over the mass of color and sound, dancing and twirling, arms aloft. The thump of the drums and bass guitar, a woman's voice singing, screaming to a crescendo. I lit a cigarette and started.

The weekend got off to a rocky start for The Lighter Than Air Fair portion of the festival when the hot air balloon became untethered from its anchor and floated away. Luckily no one was aboard the craft when it decided to take a ride all on its own. Organizers quickly alerted the FAA but many attendees were disappointed that they wouldn't get to see the sights from above.

"Hi there," a silky-smooth woman's voice said. I looked up. "Whatcha doin'?" she asked, sitting down next to me.

"Oh, hi. I'm um, well, I'm working. Working on some writing." She was pretty. Sun-kissed complexion, high cheek bones, thick raven hair, rings on her fingers, long flowery dress and Guatemalan sweater. There was a thin leather strap around her waist with a small brown purse attached to it. "Are you writing for yourself, or for that wayward balloon?" she asked, tilting her head to the east.

That's a different view point. "I guess I'm writing for myself."

"I believe that balloon didn't like being tied down," she observed, her voice sincere and warm. "It's obvious to me that it was overly starved for freedom. Just like everyone here." She quickly captured my attention.

"Good thing no one was on it. That could have been scary."

"Not for one who is seeking true freedom. It must have been ordained in the stars," she said, looking off to the west. She glanced over at my notebook and continued. "After all, everything is written in our galaxy. The stars are why everyone is here for this vibrant collage."

I gazed out over the clutch of interesting people, nodding. When something in my brain clicked, it triggered a new understanding. I saw more than just hippies and freaks. I saw a colorful vivid celebration, a painting.

"Just like you're writing, the stars are mapping the history of the universe." She stretched her legs out straight and tapped her huarache sandaled feet. "The divine galaxies affect us all, the ancients decreed it centuries ago and I believe they've brought us together to be here for this wonderful jubilee . . . most believe that we are all colored by our childhood and, that is true to some extent, but this is a place where we all can grow into ourselves."

"I can relate to that. Like a life lesson."

"Oh, yes, absolutely. It's important to understand that one's mind must learn to become independent of the social mores of society and break the bonds of ridged structure. Just like that balloon did. It freed itself all on its own. It went in search of itself, to find itself."

Just then my body tingled with pleasant energy. I set my notebook down and looked closely at her. Expressive blue eyes, bright and clear, dark eyebrows, captivating smile, but before I could respond she inquired.

"So, what are you working on? Are you a novelist?"

"I write for the Tacoma newspaper. My boss wants me to do a feature so, I need to get a feel for this," I replied, motioning to the crowd. She looked down on the festivity.

"Ooh, get a feel for it. I like that angle. So, um, do you like working for a *Tacoma*, newspaper?"

I thought about her question for a few seconds, then replied, "Well, it's kinda antiquated. But it's a paycheck."

"Ah, I see," she said, nodding. "So, what's your sign?"

"Sign?"

"Your astrological sign. You know. When were you born?"

"Oh, right," I answered, remembering what it was about. "I'm sorry, lost in the moment, I guess. I was born in December."

She chuckled to herself and smiled a beautiful smile. "Ah, the Archer in pursuit of knowledge and truth, and now, a newspaperman. What's your name?"

"I'm Cliff, McCalister, born on December 1st, 1943."

"You?"

"So, Cliff McCalister, you're a Sagittarian, that's good. I'm Allison Fisher. September 28nd, 1944. Pleased to meet you. I'm a Libra. You're Fire and I'm Air, the two go together very well, they both need something."

"What's that?"

"They need each other to survive. Fire needs oxygen."

She opened up her leather purse, pulled out a soapstone pipe and a small metal film case. She carefully opened the canister like she was uncovering an ancient crypt, her translucent eyes looking to find a new discovery of thrilling mystery or clue as to the meaning of it all. She spilled out some green leafy material into the palm of her hand like a clairvoyant. It had thin little green and red leaf's and round balled up pieces. "Have you gotten high yet today?" she asked, pulling her hair back behind her ear with a sly, roguish grin. She packed some of the stuff into the blackened bowl.

"Well, um, no I haven't," I replied. "I've never smoked marijuana, not yet anyway." She snapped her head around.

"You smoke those things," she quipped, glancing at my Winston. "Cigarettes are far, far worse for you than weed. Those things will kill you, Cliff, and weed, it's natural. It's not processed with chemicals and nicotine. Why would anyone smoke cigarettes when they don't even get you high?"

"But marijuana is illegal, and smokes aren't."

"It's certainly not illegal here — the stigma of pot is still strong with you, I see," she said, expressionless. "Well, maybe we can change that. Marijuana will allow you to connect with experiences you may never knew you could touch or appreciate . . . it allows oneself true freedom. It's a plant so completely natural that it will introduce you to a balanced level of reality that you never knew existed. There are so many unknown dimensions of reality we need to discover."

This woman had such an intoxicating presence. I was smitten with her right away. She was a sage brunette of enlightenment. "So, tell me, where're you from?"

Smiling again, she replied. "The Bay Area. I grew up in Oakland but went to San Francisco State College. My dad was a high school teacher, taught vocational ed. But I graduated with an English Lit degree."

"Journalism for me, at Gonzaga in Spokane, my dad was an accountant. But he was a big reader, loved all the classics." She flashed an understanding grin, lit her pipe and inhaled. The music blared away, guitars twanged, the drums pounded, the singers sang, and I gave-in.

Well, okay, when in Rome I guess, now act cool, Cliff.

She blew out her puff, smiled and handed the pipe to me. I clumsily grabbed it; her hands were soft and delicate. As I raised it to my mouth, she struck another match and for some unexplained reason, the sun came out from behind a cloud and shone its countenance.

I sucked in the smoke, it tasted better than my Winstons, far better. The sweet smoke filled my lungs and —

"Ahem!" Out it came, exiting my body quickly.

"That always happens the first time," she said, retrieving her pipe then tapping it on the side of the log. She placed it back in her leather pouch and said, "Your article should really take off now, and all for the better!"

"Thank you for sharing that with me. I like the taste."

"That's exactly what your article needs, a little natural effect. So, do you know of, *The Dharma Bums* by Jack Kerouac?"

"I've heard of that one. I read *On the Road* a few years ago. A copy got passed around the dorm at college."

"You did?" she replied, her eyes widening, then glowing. "I love that book, read it twice. Tell me more, what'd you think of it?"

"It's brilliant! I really enjoyed his style. It's spontaneous, like jazz, like listening to Miles Davis or Coltrane. I loved how he looked at things, the angle he takes. And Dean Moriarity, that guy was something else. Mexico was my favorite."

"Oh, I know. I loved the Mexico part too. Kerouac's an iconoclast for sure, all of them were. You should check out *Dharma Bums*, Kerouac's spiritual quest is greatly influenced by Zen Buddhism. You see, just like the characters in his books I don't want to live a life that can be easily described. I want to evoke life in everything I do and in everyone I know. I plan to eat my way through life, well, not just eat, and I don't mean eat everything. I mean to enjoy, live, love, and puff my way through every aspect of this world. Living the straight and narrow path is not for me. Narrow is too shallow, and straight, well, I only want to move forward in life and I certainly don't want to die to go to heaven. Just look around, we're already living in the Garden of Eden. It's right here. It's Shalimar," she said with a sweeping movement of her arm as she looked down on the alliance of bohemians. Then she got on her feet.

"I could use some spirituality. I'll read that Kerouac book next. So, are you here all weekend? Will I see you again?" I asked, standing up. I wanted to go with her. "Where are you going?"

"Not far," she said, grinning. "You work on your story. I'm here all weekend. I want to see you again, too, for sure. Have fun!"

"Okay, pleased to meet you, Allison. I'll see you soon," I said, smiling wide.

12:14 pm

Off she went, the most intriguing and beautiful woman I'd ever met. Medium height, slender and lissome with an athletic walk. I kept watching her as she slipped away into the music and the crowd down below. My body started tingling, and I got a warm and fuzzy feeling.

This new America wasn't defining itself like the old ways of parental values. Too boring for this bold new breed. Gone are the temperance unions, gone are the days when apple pie, ice cream, and the family radio console were enough to satisfy the palate or when Treasure Island was enough to fill the mind. The hippie youth of today looks for music and love and seeks to find true adventure.

The combined effects of marijuana and music served as a catalyst that began triggering emotions I'd never felt before. It struck a chord deep inside. Good feelings flowed through me, it felt like I was in a dreamscape, or lounging in a warm bath of soapy water, maybe watching a sultry summer sunset on the beach in a distant land. Just then I got a sudden urge of hunger, my stomach growled and my instincts said, "*Find food, now*!"

I grabbed my rucksack and dug out the turkey sandwich and took a bite – *oh my god* – food had never, ever, tasted so good. The tomato and cheese exploded in my mouth and the lettuce was so fresh and crispy. The bread, the turkey, the flavor — *holy crap, I could get used to this.* I reached for the canteen and drank deeply; the water was cool and satisfying. Then I sunk my teeth into the sandwich again with zeal and picked up my pen.

Dancing in tribal rhythm the mass of humanity moved as one, pulsating with the beat, in tune with the vibrations of the rock music, together they all became brothers and sisters of the sun in a shared life affirming moment in time, their time. Because these vagabonds of the youth movement care about each other in ways this reporter has never seen before. Helpful, happy, and present.

"Come on, man. Hurry up!" someone said, walking by. I raised my head and saw a group of people heading into the woods behind me. Three guys and two girls scampering in earnest, their destination unknown. I looked down upon the ever-growing mass of hair and humanity, took in the music, and gathered my thoughts.

The power in the music doesn't just come from an electric guitar amplified enough to be heard in outer space, the true power of music is the power it has to connect people in a primordial instinct that we humans need to survive. Music is like church, a place to worship and be baptized, take fellowship, albeit unorthodox, the refrain is not only that, but a trigger to unleash the long tether of life that once held these youth to the established —

"Whoo-hoo!"

"Awesome!"

"Come on in!" I heard coming from up the hill behind me. I stopped writing and got up to see what was happening.

A short distance away, I came upon a dozen naked bodies swimming and splashing in what looked like an irrigation pond set in the middle of a grove of cedar trees. A small concrete dam imbedded in the water with a gate valve and pipe headed downhill. Surrounded with ferns, boulders, and rocks around the rim of it, the sun shone down on the revelers, all of them naked to the world, in natural, communal bliss.

One woman came walking up out of the water right in front of me, her wet naked body glistening in the sun, a beaded necklace dangling between her tan lined breasts. She stepped up out of the pond like I wasn't there, then bent over and picked up a towel. As she was drying herself off another woman, buxom and blonde got out — *What?* — it was the girl from the day before.

"Hey buddy!" one of the guys yelled at me, "are you comin' in or just gonna stare at my girlfriend?!"

"Shit!" another fella hollered. "That's the reporter guy! The investigator!"

"Either jump in and join us, or get yer eyeballs gone!"

Feeling high and a touch self-conscience, I raised my hand and said, "That's okay, I was just wondering what all the yelling and noise was about. That's all."

Coming back into the gathering I saw Cyrus. He was in front of the Orange Sunshine $1 shirtless sign guy. "I don't care if you're using that stuff, but you can't be sitting around with a cardboard ad selling it." He took the sign, ripped it in half and glared at him while the stoned-out hippie didn't move a muscle. But his transfixed eyes changed to the look of shock and surprise then he croaked, "Aw man." Cyrus turned on his heel and left.

Buddha came over the sound system. "Okay boys and girls! Are you ready for some good old protest music! Are you ready to tell all those politicians in DC that you're sick and tired of our boys over in Nam! Yeah, well, let's all give a hand for one of the originals! All the way from Haight-Ashbury in San Francisco! Here they are! It's time for Country Joe and The Fish!"

1:13 pm

In the short amount of time that I'd been gone, gazing upon the beauty and wonders of the natural world, the festival had grown into a small village encampment of tents, lean-tos, and assorted living arrangements. As the stage came into view I could see five musicians, one out front had an acoustic guitar, the crowd had pushed forward, right to the stage.

"Gimme an F!" the singer cried out. "F!" the crowd shouted back with glee. "Gimme a U!" "U!" On he went with spelling out the word, fuck. "What's that spell?" he finally asked and the crowd hollered back with a gigantic earth-shaking acknowledgement, "Fuck!"

Uncle Sam needs help, There's some jam in Vietnam, We need to drop our books and pick up guns, It will be so much fun when we get killed and end up in a casket, Watch out or you're going to be in Vietnam, The Gates of Heaven are going to open up and there wasn't time to wonder about it, Because everyone was gonna die.

With each step I got closer to the stage and the enormous mass of people. Kids, men, women, freaks, short hair, long hair, beads, flowers, sandals, dogs, bare feet, ankle bracelets, bells, clapping, and singing. At the first open spot of grass, I sat down, got out my paper and pen, put my head down and started in.

The whole crowd sang along with Country Joe & The Fish, every word. I'd never seen or heard anything like it before. It was an amazing sight to see, witness and hear. Everyone in unison, singing their hearts out against the war, making their statement out loud for the country side and the country itself to hear. One big rejection of Uncle Sam. I was wonderfully stunned and proud and agreed with every single one of them. I was no fan of the war and now, after seeing this massive display I was proud to be here and be a part of this important gathering of true freedom with no boundaries, no inhibitions. These bold and epic voyagers were believers in the freedom of choice, the freedom to go and do what one wanted, to break free from all the rules and make their own, and lose all constraints. All of them partners, not just with each other, but partners with the music, with the band, and the band was partners with them. They are all in it together, together as one, a combined entity of peace and tranquility.

I stopped, looked up and noticed right away that there were a good number of Native

Americans intermingled in the dancing crowd. Doing Native steps and moves, all of them smiling brightly and laughing. Then I remembered seeing the poster at the ticket line, the one about all profits going to Native American Organizations. It was a beautiful sight to see so many different people, black, white, Native, Asian, Latino, and all of them American. All races side by side in living harmony. I was about to start in again but the enticing aroma of grilled beef came wafting through the air.

Following my nose, I spotted a hamburger stand. An ad hoc kiosk of lumber with a brown metal roof. Smoke and flames shot up from greasy donated family grills, Weber's, Sears, and charcoal, all manned by women of the earth. Long dresses, beads, flowers behind ears and enough of that same sweet-scented perfume that I noticed on the Portland gang the day before. *What is that?* And just as right as rain, there was Raoul, sitting on a stump nearby chomping away on a burger. He was by himself so I thought I'd join him, but first, I was hungry again, and in dire need of sustenance.

"Burger or hotdog?" a woman said, wiping the sweat from her brow with her forearm, looking tired. She wore a homemade dress fashioned out of bib overalls.

"How about a hotdog, please," I replied, reaching in my pocket for some change.

"You want sprouts on that?" she asked, turning dogs.

"Sprouts?"

"Alfalfa sprouts — they're a good source of vitamins and anti-oxidants."

I saw a big bowl filled with thin green shoots next to her, they didn't look very appealing. *Geez, that looks awful.*

"How about some ketchup and mustard, onion maybe?"

She nodded and slapped together my bun and hotdog and wrapped it up in a piece of red and white wax paper.

"Twenty-five cents," she said, holding out her hand and then pointing, "everything else you need is over there."

“Thanks.” I dropped a quarter in her hand. Once I’d slathered my hotdog with the appropriate condiments I walked over to Raoul.

“Hey, how are ya’ doing? Whatcha think of this crazy hippie party?”

“Welcome to the feel-good bash of the year!” he said with a smile. “These folks up here really know how to stomp on the terra! Boy, oh boy! La Honda’s got nothing on these people. This is the real deal, very organic, and completely authentic,” he said in between bites. *La Honda? What’s he talking about? Riding a Honda isn’t better than this? Even I know that!* But he had an odd way of speaking, in a kind of halting and erratic, stuttering under his breath way.

“Yes, they do.” I bit into the hotdog and looked out over the crowd. A long line of people had joined hands with one shirtless man in cut-off jeans and long hair leading them in a wild serpentine string of chain dancers weaving their way through the mass of other dancers in front of the stage while Country Joe sang.

He was singing about going to the LA airport, How somebody stuck some money in his hand so he could pay for his flight getting home, And he was flying high all the way home, Stoned the whole time on weed.

"Can you believe how a modern sound system of this size can project every note out into these woods and be heard for miles around? What a show!" he observed. "These stoned out freaks have every right to have their own kind of freedom, and plenty of reasons to let off a little steam. They've got every right on the planet to frolic and be happy in this fucked up world," he said, motioning at the dancers, spinning and twirling, as the long line of snaking dancers ran around and through the crowd.

"Absolutely."

"Especially after that rat bastard Daley beat the living hell out us in Chicago earlier this week," he said, shaking his head. "Welp, I gotta go. Got a plane to catch."

"You're leaving? Right now? There's two more days."

"Nope, gotta go. I've already missed the first flight, got too much junk to deal with back home. It was good to meet you, Cliff. Good luck!" *Wow, he remembered my name. I wonder if it's about that phone call last night*?

"You, too," I replied, sticking out my hand. He shook it firmly and then walked off through the gathering. The man's awkward gait was odd with his feet pointing outward as he stepped and made erratic arm movements while turning his head from side to side getting one last look. I wondered again. *Who is he*?

"Let's hear it one more time for Country Joe and The Fish," Buddha hollered into the microphone. "Country Joe everybody, Country Joe and The Fish! Next up we've got Santana! They've came all the way up from San Francisco to be here today and they are gonna blow your mind. So, get ready people! Get ready to shake and rattle your bones! In the meantime, we've got good eats over at the concession area. Burgers and hotdogs for twenty-five cents and remember people let's stay cool and be kind to your brother!"

In front of the land owners house there was a long line of heads and freaks waiting to fill jugs and bottles at the well because someone decided it was a good time to wash their hair. Big lines were backed-up at the SaniKan's and people were still arriving by the dozens, showing up from the main entrance and coming through the trees, all of them searching for a camping spot. Then I spied John Chambless walking towards the food kiosk.

Walking over to him I said, “John, hey John,” raising my hand and smiling. He looked at me and nodded.

“Would you have any time for a quick question?”

“Sure, but I don’t have much. I just got word that our charter bus broke down near Woodinville.”

“Holy smokes! It did?”

“Yep, they think the fuel pump blew. So now we have to go to our back-up shuttle plan with our volunteers.”

“Gosh, that’s too bad. So, I wanted to ask you about the non-profit and donations going to Native American Organizations.”

“Yes, well,” he replied, reaching for a hotdog, “all the money will be distributed to many different Native tribes and their affiliated groups. Only the musicians will be making any profits from this. Myself and Cyrus, who is a good friend of mine, we mortgaged our homes to raise the capital to put this little soiree on. What do you think so far?" He was slightly built and had a southern drawl in his voice.

"Well," I replied, looking him in the eye, "it's the best darn music festival I've ever been to. That's for sure."

"So far so good, that is, except for the balloon getting away and now with the bus breaking down."

"Yes, um, what do you think will happen with the balloon?"

"We called the FAA about it and found a balloonist in Spokane who is heading west with his truck to try and find it. That's about all we can do at this time."

"And what about the MC's comment about the Beatles?"

"Oh, boy. I don't know how to respond to that. I think he gets a little too carried away with himself." He swallowed a bite of his hotdog and then said, "I've got to get back. We'll talk again." We shook hands while he nodded at me and quickly walked away.

3:27 pm

Buddha turned up his microphone. "Okay, folks! Let's hear it for Santana!"

A drummer, another with congas and cymbals, a white organist with an afro, a black man on bass, and an olive-skinned guy with black hair and goatee stood with a small red guitar. He hit one long note, loud and sustained. He held that note long enough for the soundwave to bounce off Seattle, then waited for it to ebb back. Like a call to arms, a battle cry, a reveille. He struck another, the emotion on his face clearly visible, eyes closed, mouth open, it echoed out over the crowd and into the hills. Then the conga guy began to beat a fast rhythm, setting the tempo, writing the time signature, replying to the guitarist's opening statement. Next the drummer responded, answering his call with a powerful cadence, and BOOM! The bass joined in and they take off like a rocket. Driving, pounding Latin pulsating rhythms. *Wow*! Everyone leapt to their feet, cheering, dancing, going wild with rebellious abandon, like they'd all been overtaken and seized by a force bigger than the trees and mountains that surrounded them. *Who the hell are these guys and why haven't I heard of them*? On and on they went.

Building the song, climbing to crescendos, then back to the main melody, searching, playing off of each other, improvising, each musician watching the other, driving, pounding, while the crowd's going crazy, arms in the air, twirling, jumping, spinning, cheering, clapping, heaving with the music and the conga rhythms beating in their ears, beating in their hearts, sounding out to the world. All instrumental, all moving, all encompassing, all enveloping, passionate, sexy music that was otherworldly. In a stream of consciousness, the notes flowed from his guitar like Iberian poetry. *This is like Barcelona meets Rock-n-Roll!*

If someone told me that faith was a belief in the unseen I would have laughed because the reaction from the crowd was visual, palpable, visceral. I could feel the music and see what the music did. Pushing, pulsating, living, breathing, giving, discovering. The music covered me and everyone else in lava, like syrup. Steaming and hot, pouring over everyone in a life affirming moment. Soaking all of us, sinking into the marrow. If this was anarchy, then I wanted more . . . a whole lot more!

The smoke of marijuana billowed above the crowd and hung like stubborn coastal fog, settling in, indignant, not leaving for any unlawful reason. We will not be denied the sweet vapors told the world. Neither will we spoke the dancers. This is our time, we will change the world, we will do things our way! We will do it now!

The driving rhythms from the percussion section of the San Francisco band, Santana, threw the crowd into a wild frenzy of Latin rock music, bringing the crowd to its feet in an amazing display of unity, freedom and culture. The power that the band was generating was beyond belief. Pushing, pulsating, pounding drums and bass against my chest like a living breathing musical animal, alive and living in the moment, giving . . . discovering . . . sharing the power of music. Drums of thunder, crashing cymbals of lightning, the thump —

Looking up, the music pounded but so did the same sleeping bag I saw earlier in the woods, right in front of me. Up and down, it went. But this time there was a circle of people around it, all of them, men and women, cheering along, dancing, throwing their heads back in delight, urging them on, some of them embracing and kissing, running off into the forest — love children.

When in Rome . . . It was out of the ordinary to witness for me, a person raised in Spokane from a conservative household, all staunch Republicans who would be alarmed. But for some unexplained reason, I was loving it. The band had shifted gears and the organist was singing.

There's an evil woman with bad ways, His girlfriend, Something has to change, Or they're going to stop, He was tired because she'd been running around, His baby needs to change.

A white man with long uncombed hair, all of it hanging in clumps wearing a cotton shirt with bright colored stripes, yellow, red, blue, and orange appeared before me. He smiled a happy smile and held out a giant marijuana cigarette. "Have some grass, man, it's the herb of life and good for the spirit." His smile was so sincere, big white chompers, one tooth had a gold band. *What the hell, why not.* I'd already lost the warm and fuzzy feeling from before. I reached out and took hold of it in an automatic response. Sucking in some of the smoke it tasted far different from what Allison had. Thick and heavy, earthy and dank. Handing it back, I instantly started coughing, hard.

"You'll be okay, man, you'll be good for the day now."

"Okay — sure. Ahem! Thanks." My whole body started to buzz, far more than earlier. The warm and fuzzy feeling began to intensify and the music filled my soul with emotions and thoughts I'd never had before. Looking around at my surroundings I didn't see hippies, or Heads, or even a crowd of people. I saw an ancient ritual, a coming together of tribes, a family, a clan. A genuine community where people could feel that they belonged, not only in their world, but to each other. Beautiful people, all of them, celebrating life and all of its experiences. True love, no exclusions, no limits, no boundaries in a display of complete impartiality and unification. I raised my sights to take in the forest and the natural world and saw a red-tailed hawk, watching us from a dead tree snag, regal and majestic. I'd never seen a hawk in that way before, always just as a bird.

In a flash of consciousness, I realized that The Hawk was the most important thing there was. I became insignificant. An understanding came over me, an understanding that the natural environment was far more important than anything else. The survival of that Hawk and all wild species was way more important than everything. In an instant, I felt gratitude for our planet. I grabbed my backpack and walked over to the base of the dead snag, sat down below the stoic bird and took out my pen and notebook.

Take notice! Take notice! Look at me! Look at us! The human race is a walking conundrum. We walk erect, have big brains and even bigger appetites, not just for food but for extracting resources from our earth, the Hawk's earth. I must separate ego from myself. The human race must dispel its ego. Even though we have the largest amount of brain matter and frontal lobe and . . . we speak . . . and make . . . zz . . . zzz . . . zzzzz . . . grand . . . zzzzzzzzz . . . mistakes —

6:15 pm

Hours later I came too. Sitting up straight I glanced around and then rubbed my eyes. *What on earth*?!? My notebook and rucksack were right beside me and another band was on stage, sounding good. Everyone was seated now, laid back and the sun had dropped. I'd been in a deep, satisfying sleep, it seemed like I'd dreamt I was flying. *Man, oh, man. That was some strong stuff that guy had.* It felt like it was time to head back to town. I stood up and carefully scanned the whole festival for Allison, but didn't see her, then kept watching for her on my way out.

On the berry bus, there were a few other riders but no Jake or Adam. I couldn't even remember seeing them at the gathering, maybe they got the same feel-good vibe that I did. Who knows, perhaps the big learning curve ball was thrown at them, too. A real-life learning event that happened to change their lives.

The bus driver closed the door and off we went, but straight ahead, then we turned and the driver said over his shoulder, "Just a quick stop up at the campground and then back to Sultan and your cars."

I felt drained, but completely satisfied, happy. Gazing out the window I thought back on the day and told myself how wrong I was about not wanting to take on the assignment, thinking it was going to be a waste of time. When, up ahead, in a small pasture there was . . . *is that a tipi?* The driver wheeled into the campground and followed a circular dirt path then stopped to let some passengers off. Nobody got on so he started to drive away. Going slow we approached the tipi and the buses I saw the day before, along with a couple of VW vans, some cars and tents. The two buses had hung tarps between them where chairs, tables, and a seating area was set up. But what really caught my eye was the tipi. For some unexplained reason it captured my attention, it looked so natural with its brown canvas covering and poles coming out the top resting in the meadow-like field. A toddler in diapers ran about and some laundry was hanging while two women in long dresses kept themselves busy with smiles on their faces, looking healthy, looking happy.

There's Allison!! She was walking towards the buses and tipi. I quickly pulled the window open, stuck my head out and hollered, "Hey Allison! Is that you? See you tomorrow!"

She snapped her head around and waved, "Cliff! Where were you?" Come by here in the morning!"

As the bus rolled by, I hollered back, "Yes! I will! Yes!"

Sportsman's Café

Back in town, the Pass Time was packed to the rafters with beer swilling Sultanites, country music blared away. Babbling people came and went while across the street, the café was busy but quiet. My ears were still ringing from the day, a peaceful beer and some hot comfort food was just what I needed.

A thin bank of cigar and cigarette smog diminished visibility and stunk; it was awful. *Geez, weed smells a lot better than this!* While social banter of the festival fell from every lumberjack's mouth like heavy timber hitting the forest floor. Booths with wrinkled and cracked brown naugahyde seating ran along the window, a mahogany counter with chrome stools, rough wood flooring, and in the background hushed tones from the jukebox delivered a country lament. *Mama wore a short-skirt and then put the PTA in its place.*

Every wall was plastered with framed photos of men holding up trophy sized steelhead or trout, mounted deer and elk heads, and a giant stuffed king crab hung across the wall behind the counter, shiny from layers of shellac.

Still bleary eyed and slightly buzzed from my marijuana encounter earlier in the day all the chatter stopped and heads turned as I took a seat at the counter. Just like the night before, everything returned to normal once I was accepted. I grabbed a menu from the salt and pepper station that ran along the back of the counter while silverware clanged and the cook hollered, "Order up!"

"What'll you have?" a woman's voice asked. She was young, maybe college age, downcast eyes, her brown hair done in a flip. By outward appearances I assumed the bulk of her hard-earned paychecks were spent on make-up.

"Can I get a cold bottle of Heidelberg and the pot roast special?"

"Sorry, no beer, no alcohol," she said, looking at me without comprehension. "You'll have to go across the street for that. We have coffee, or water, milk maybe?"

"No beer?"

"Yep, the owner doesn't allow it. He's very strict," she replied, tapping her pad with a stubby pencil. "And pretty grumpy about what's going on with the rock festival."

"Really?"

"Oh, yeah."

"Okay, well, water's fine then."

The jukebox crooned over a couple's impending divorce becoming a finality that will impact the couple's young son.

"Vivian, I'm telling you this hippie thing is never gonna happen here again. I don't care how much money all the business owners are making. We can't have the kids of this town being influenced by a bunch of drug taking, draft dodging pacifists' year in and year out. There's no way we can ever let this mistake continue. Besides, there's too much traffic, we just had to walk three blocks when we usually park in front."

“Oh gosh, there you go again, complaining about having to walk. And those hippie kids are no threat to you or anyone else. Just because they look at life with a different set of eyes than you, it doesn’t mean we can’t prosper from this. What are you gonna do when all the old growth timber is gone? You can’t log forever.”

“The hell we can’t! Everyone’s gonna keep livin’ in houses built outta wood ya’ know. Weyerhaeuser’s been replanting and the timber is still gonna flow to the mills. Forever.”

“Lloyd, this town needs something else besides logging that will sustain itself for the years to come. The world is changing and our town is going to die off if it doesn’t create some other industry for the future. Quit being so bullheaded. Mary Jane told me that she and her sister went to the Roxy in Everett last weekend and saw that new *Space Odessey* movie. She said there was a computer on board a spaceship that turned into a human brain with its own thoughts and ideas and took it over! Things are changing Lloyd. Someday someone is going to invent a faster typewriter, and better phones, plus, there’ll be robots, and flying cars. Just like on the *Jetson’s* and *Star Trek* and computers like in that movie. Sultan’s going to need to keep up with the world and we need to be ready."

Heartache and heartbreak, Sleepless nights, How Long Will My Baby Be Gone? The singer wanted to know.

"Ha! *The Jetson's* and *Star Trek!* And Computers!?!" he scoffed. "I don't believe in any of that science fiction mumbo jumbo! I say we go out there and wipe the slate clean. Get those damn hippies outta here. Why I heard Henry caught some of 'em last night stealing apples and pulling carrots out of his garden! Nothing but a bunch of takers and thieves. I just don't understand these kids today! Don't they have homes to go to and real lives to live?"

"Stop it, Lloyd. Just because you don't understand them it doesn't mean they're all bad. Why, I do recall the time you and Orvil stole, or should I say like you, *borrowed,* his dad's chainsaw while he was out of town and cut cord wood all weekend back when you were in high school. It's not like you've never done wrong."

"That's different, Viv —"

"It most certainly is not. You didn't have permission to use that saw, and, if I remember correctly, you two used up all his dad's gas and bar oil. Get off your high horse."

"Yeah, well, at least we weren't using drugs or laying around all day watching the grass grow. All these kids wanna do is skip through the flowers all day. They're far worse than we ever were. Why're you takin' sides?"

"I'm not taking sides. Those folks aren't hurting anyone. Kids today are under a lot more pressure than we ever were what with the war and the draft and all the protests and riots. I think they've got a right to speak their peace. After all our young boys in Vietnam can kill, but they can't even vote. What's right in that?"

"Them hippies out at Betty's are a bunch of draft dodging bums, and that's all I got to say about it —"

"Here you go," the waitress said, setting down my dinner.

"Thanks. So, um, tell me, are you from around here?"

"Oh yeah. Born down in Monroe. Lived here all my life."

"And, so, does everyone in Sultan work in the woods or the mills?"

"Pretty much. My dad drives log truck and my brother sets choke. Uncle John works at Mill B in Everett."

Hmm, sets choke? Mill B? Whatever that all means?

"So, did you get a chance to go out and listen to some music today?" I asked, poking at my meal with a dull knife and a thin fork.

"Not a chance. And work for Judge Boyle? Oh, gosh no, he'd have a conniption if I went out there. I gotta go, he needs more coffee." And off she went around the corner to the dining room.

XI

Day Two

Was I swimming underwater? Or was I flying? How is this happening? The air is thick like water but yet, I'm dry and doing the breaststroke over the trees below, breathing water like air — soaring now with my arms at my side, kicking my feet then turning down and seeing a river with snowcapped mountains in the distance. And . . . music, beautiful music filling my heart, filling my soul, dousing me with a balmy flood of notes —

Turning over from a deep sleep I rubbed my eyes. *Where was I?* The alarm clock didn't even go off. It was 7:34. No Raoul, no screeching, no electric typewriter, just peace and quiet all night. Outside I could hear the wind.

Sideways stiletto rain slashed through the air. Pools of water dotted the parking lot and dark clouds covered the sky. *Good thing I brought a rain coat.* For some unexplained reason it reminded me of my dad, always calling wet weather 'Irish mist' saying things like; 'It's bucketing down' and if it was lightly raining, he'd say, 'There's a soft rain today.' Stormy days seemed to remind me of so many things about him. Once in a while he'd get upset with me and we'd quarrel. He had his reasons but Dad always meant well. I still love him though; he wanted the very best for my brother and me.

After a shower I got dressed and strapped on my hiking boots then reached for the pack of Winston's but stopped. *Allison doesn't like those and I'm not so sure I do anymore either*— and left them. Inside the café, no Raoul and massive breakfast, just some locals having a Sunday morning meal, coffee, and talk.

"When I got up last night, I could hear that damn rock-n-roll music all the way down here in town. At three a.m.! And here we've got two more days! I don't believe it."

"Oh, Hank," his wife said. "It wasn't that bad, I didn't hear a thing, slept right through the whole night. Maybelle Koons said their market did really good business the last few days. She said the kids were all well-mannered and Ernie's Market sold out, I heard."

"Aw. They're just a bunch draft card burning druggies. Drop-outs every single one of them. Well mannered? Ha!"

"Morning Sugar," Doreen said. "Are you here all weekend?"

"I am. Covering the big festival for the paper I work for."

"No kidding. So, you're a newspaper reporter then?"

"Yep, the last year and a half," I replied, looking over the menu. "I think I'll have the Denver omelette with some bacon and coffee."

"Morning, Hank. Morning, Millie," a man said to the couple, walking in with his wife. "Millie, it's good to see you today," his spouse said in an upbeat tone. She glanced over at Millie's husband, just nodded, saying in a monotone voice, "Hank."

"So?" Hank started, looking at his friend, "whatcha thing about this mess?"

"It's a damn shame we never shoulda let this thing happen."

"Bill, you know the town tried to stop it and we couldn't. So now we just have to make the best of it," Millie replied. "It's good for business. They're money spends just as good as anyone else's. It'll be fine."

"Who says it's good for business? Who told you that story?"

"Why Maybelle Koons said so, Bill. Said her market is taking in money hand over fist. And all the kids are cordial."

"Aw, phooey. That's a big old slice of baloney. I don't believe it for a single second — Hank?"

"I'm with you, Bill. I don't like it one bit. Not at all."

For the next twenty minutes all I wanted to do was stand up and tell those two old men that Millie was right. But I didn't. It wasn't was my place. It was their town. They'd probably been here all their lives, owned homes, raised their kids, paid their taxes. They had the right to say what they felt. Just like we did.

8:57 am

At the shuttle lot in town, I was amazed to see license plates from all across the country; Vermont, New York, Virginia, Texas, and California. On the ride out to the festival the bus was full but the sky was dishwater gray, a steady drizzle pelted the windshield but it didn't diminish attendance. Hundreds of cars were parked on the side of the road and a host of festival goers, some in raincoats, others without, walked beside the right-of-way undeterred in their quest. At the festival entrance, everyone got off the bus except me.

"You headed up to the campground?" the driver asked.

"Yes, please."

A few minutes later I stepped off and turned to look at the tipi encampment. Smoke curled from the stovepipes that jutted upward from each bus roof, it was a peaceful, natural sight. The colors on the one bus seemed to shine from all the moisture and I was torn. *Should I go over there in search of her*? I'm sure they wouldn't mind if I knocked on their door. Everyone's been so friendly.

As I got closer, I noticed the blue license plates. *Oregon, hmm.* Then 10-feet away I hesitated, second thoughts came over me when the door on the multi-colored bus opened and a man with well-combed red hair and a closely trimmed beard came out with a grin saying, "Good morning."

"Hi, um. I'm sorry to bother you. But I met a woman yesterday, Allison. She asked me to come by this morning; might she be staying here? I saw her, she —"

"You must be the writer," he replied, smiling brightly.

"She's next door, with her sister and brother in-law."

Window curtains moved on the green bus and I could hear movement inside, a brief commotion, when the door opened wide and a smiling Allison jumped out.

"Cliff!"

"Hi, Allison. I hope this is okay? You said for me to come by in the morning. So, here I am." She walked right straight at me and then gave me a big hug.

"It's so good to see you. Where did you go yesterday?"

"Oh, gosh. It's a long story. I, well, I took a nap."

"What? You took a nap? How? With all that music?"

"I know . . . I know. Like I said, it's a long story."

"You better come in and meet everybody," she said, grinning. "But the kids are still asleep, we have to be quiet."

Surrounded by calming soft Irish mist, I followed her over to the bus and silently up the stairs inside. There was a woman standing at a sink wearing a white sleeping gown, long black hair in a ponytail and bare feet. Across from her a man was laying on a sofa in cutoffs, reading a book, his legs stretched out nearly the length of the couch. His hair was long, but not like hippie long, kind of Errol Flynn-esk, straight back, and he wore a pair of wire-rimmed glasses. He looked up from his reading and then stood with a gracious welcoming smile.

“Hi, I’m Darren. Allison mentioned you last night. And this is my wonderful wife and Alli’s sister, Teresa.”

“Hi Cliff, good to meet you,” she replied with a grin. “Alli told us all about how you’re here to do a feature article for your newspaper. That’s so cool.”

I shook hands with both of them and said, quietly, “Yes, I am. But I’ve got a long way to go and people keep —”

“People keep getting you high,” Allison added with a cute little simper. Everybody chuckled under their breath.

“So, Allison,” Teresa whispered, “you need to come back in another couple of hours. You’ve got babysitting duty so we can have some music time, too. And Cliff, your job for today is to get her back on time.”

“Absolutely.”

“Okay, great. That would be great. I like you already.”

Allison tied a blue bandana around her head and wore a pair of circular earrings with beads;

she looked like a pirate queen. I instantly melted inside. Then she slipped on a tan rain coat as I stepped towards the door. She gave her sister and Darren a hug. I raised my hand and quietly said, "See you in a little while."

"Let's just walk, the shuttle won't be back for a long time and it's less than a mile. It's good to walk."

9:32 am

Then Buddha's voice boomed out over the sound system. "Good morning Sky River! Okay, let's hear it for the opening act of the day! The New Lost City Ramblers! All the way from Greenwich Village, The New Lost City Ramblers! Give 'em a hand everybody! Let's hear it!"

"Thank you, thank you! This first one's called Breadline Blues. We hope you like it."

The rich make the rules that create breadlines, They're no joke, Everyone has been robbed with no money left only a corn cob in the breadline, That's the blues.

Wearing blue jeans and leather boots her raven hair framed her face below her bandana. *She's so beautiful.* We stepped into the soft mist and Allison pulled the hood over her head. Then she asked, “What happened to you yesterday?”

“Oh gosh. I, well, this guy who had long matted hair that hung in clumps stuck a big old joint in front of me and I took a puff. I guess I’m a hippie now, maybe.”

“Haha!” she laughed, “Let’s not get to ahead of ourselves. How about we go with proto-hippie, for now. But one with great potential. And so?”

“Oh, okay. Proto-hippie it is. Anyway, I took a puff and it tasted different than what you had. It was obviously a lot stronger and it made me feel really good and I saw the world so much differently.” Allison flashed her same roguish grin from the day before, thinking to herself.

“Cool.”

“Then I saw this hawk in a dead tree snag, and I’d never seen a hawk look so regal and important like that before. It was an astonishing thing. I’d always just looked at birds like they were only birds and that they didn’t matter. Well, I mean, I know they matter, but I’d never understood how beautiful they were, all birds and creatures, that pot he had made the natural so much more profound."

"Good. And then?"

"Well, I went over to the snag, sat down, and started writing. I got about a paragraph written and fell asleep. That stuff just knocked me out, simple as that." Allison started giggling and then gave me a little hug.

"That is so cute. I think he had some indica, you need to stick with sativa, if you can. It's not as strong but it's still euphoric."

"Indica?"

"They're two strains of marijuana. Indica is usually more potent, that stuff puts me on the couch every time and I try to stay away from it. There needs to be some way us potheads can determine which is which besides by smoking it."

A woman bundled in warm clothes was holding an umbrella over herself at the entrance, she glanced at our tickets when we showed them. With a wave of her hand, we walked the gentle hill and came to find ourselves in the middle of a giant field of mud.

"Holy mother of . . . what a sight! Look at this place!"

"The rain really pounded the bus last night, and these people."

It's early in the morning, Working so hard for too little money, The man says go on strike, But it doesn't pay.

The matted down grass from the day before combined with the rain and had turned the ground into a big oozy mess. The folks that stayed the night were now waterlogged, their tents and lean-tos soggy, but most still had the same smiles as the day before. However, one fellow that went by us looked like a walking cadaver, pale white, gaunt, and with his eyes straight ahead. Wrapped in a dirty blanket, he looked as if he'd already reached his nadir. Two women saw him at the same time, they went over and comforted him, talking softly, then led him away to the safety of the open-door clinic.

A visqueen roof had been built over the stage and one for the soundboard. More plywood had been fastened to the underpinnings of the stage, and with the white linen for a backdrop, it gave the whole affair a finished, professional look. As we glanced around, Allison asked, "So, Cliff. Tell me, what are you looking for in life?"

I thought about her question. *Is this a test?* Then said, "I want to be happy in life and fulfilled, but money's never been my driver. I mean, I know we need it to survive but I'm not going to chase after things that only money can buy. I know we all need it to get by but literature, mostly the classics, have held my interest on the whole. I love words and language, and ideas. Love to read and write, build sentences with interesting and entertaining combinations of words."

"Okay, very cool. So, tell me, what's your favorite word then?"

"Hilarious."

"Really?"

"Oh, yeah. Because it's *hilarious* and I love to laugh."

"Yours?"

"Well it used to be, nuance. But now I believe my favorite word is, love."

"Love?"

"Yes, love," she remarked, glancing at me with her expressive blue eyes and warm smile. "Because love is everything, it's all encompassing and such a powerful word."

"But it used to be, nuance. Why nuance?"

"Oh, I don't know. I guess I liked the sound of it. It's so subtle, and kind of shaded in a way. I like how it rolls off the tongue. Say it, *nuance.* And you'll see."

"*Nuance*," I repeated, then smiled. "Oh, yeah, I get it. I like it, but I like your new favorite word better."

Allison grinned an infectious grin and then we looked out over the eclectic crowd of people and their make do arrangements.

I noticed a new group of people off to the front of the stage. One fellow had a small black cowboy hat on his head and a Levi jacket with a dark turtleneck sweater underneath. He looked sophisticated, like a dapper cowboy with a lopsided handlebar moustache. The guy next to him wore a long orange tunic with buttons. They were smiling and carrying on like sailors.

"Do you have a girlfriend?" Allison ventured, right out of the blue. But it didn't surprise me.

"Nope. I did during college though, but she left for a job on the east coast. We didn't stay in touch." Allison put her hands in the pockets of her coat, staying quiet. It felt like she wanted me to say more. *This is a test!*

"She was kinda quiet, and didn't like my friends, what few I had. But they were good guys and they had girlfriends too. It's just that, she wasn't very talkative or outgoing."

"And you're outgoing, that is?" she blurted out, then it seemed like she started to say something but stopped.

"Go on, what is it? Do you think I'm a homebody?"

"Oh, no. Not at all. You're here at a rock festival after all. It's not that, I just, well, I like to look at life through a different kind of lens, a technicolor lens. Darren believes that good and evil walk hand in hand and that you can't have one without the other. Like the yin and yang. I believe that yang, being the light in the world, is where I want to reside and I know that balance is important, too. Steve on the other hand, he thinks that if one only looks at the world through rose colored glasses then you'll eventually either have your glasses broken or stolen and then one would be, well, out of luck. He can be very energetic and I like that about him. If you get him going, Steve can be pretty vocal and opinionated about things. He's concerned about the environment right now and always means good, he's a good friend, someone you can count on."

"They both sound like interesting people. But what about you? Do you have a boyfriend? I mean, you're here alone and I don't want to assume anything."

"I did, but I don't. He was a handsome guy, like you, but a Scorpio, very secretive and way too intense for me."

"Let's hear it for The New Lost City Ramblers!" Buddha hollered. After the applause died down a few in the crowd began to heckle him.

"Hey man! Where's the Beatles? You said yesterday they were gonna be here today. Where are they?"

"Yeah, no shit. Where's the Beatles? Huh? Mr. Buddha!"

"I'm workin' on it! Wouldn't that be great to have Paul McCartney sing, *Good Day Sunshine*, today! We could sure use it! But now we've got Dino Valenti!" Buddha announced. "He's got his acoustic guitar and is going to sing for us. Here he is," he added as the singer walked on stage. Holding a 12-string dreadnought guitar Valenti sauntered on stage, his thick black curly hair down in his eyes. He stepped up to the mic and strummed his instrument a few times and then gazed out over the crowd.

"How's everybody doin' after last night?" he asked to faint cheers. "It looks like it's not going to let up but who knows, maybe we'll get some sunshine today. Here's one I wrote years ago that the Youngbloods recorded on their first album. Thanks Jesse and Lowell. I just wanted to do it first today!" he pronounced, glancing backstage. "Okay, here we go folks."

Love is a song we all know, And the foothills ring, Angels crying, Bird's flying, People should treat one another with kindness and smile for everyone, Love each other right away, Every day.

The song's message got through to the crowd, many of them rising to their feet and swaying to the music, muddy and wet, most smiling, some singing along. As we stood enjoying the music an older Indian man trundled by. He had a hand-made blackened walking stick with a carved eagle head; the shaft whittled like a totem pole. Long gray hair, blue shirt and beaded necklace with a fringed brown leather coat. He was magnificent.

"What a beautiful man," Allison said, once he passed.

"He looked like a wise man, or a chief the way he carried himself. I bet he's part of the Native American Organizations who are the beneficiaries of this little soiree."

Allison nodded in agreement. After a short pause she observed, "The people here are just as much the stars of this festival as the musicians and performers are."

"Absolutely, this is like a human hipster bazaar . . . how about if we walk around, take in the sights?"

10:46 am

Floating vapors of white mist slid over the treetops as if they knew right where they were going, to Sky River to sing a water song. The soaking rain knocking on the roof of every tent and visqueen hovel in a flourish of notes. It drenched the audience with love and cleansing, the rain gathering in the muddy footprints of rainbow wishing soldiers, it filled their blissful consciousness with hopes and dreams of change.

Allison led the way around the edge of the gathering against the tree line. The ancient conifers watched as we climbed the perimeter, they stood tall, waiting for time, their limbs waving at us in the breeze. Over squishy ground, we made our way past all types of bivouacked youth, some had smoldering fires for cooking, others still in sleeping bags under tents and copious other arrangements. The soft ground of the farm had drunk as much rain as it could. The soil was too tired to accept anymore, it could no longer agree with the cloud's argument.

As we approached a sagging brown tent a long-haired bleary-eyed fellow crawled out, followed by two more. The first one stood yawning and stretching his arms, straightening his back, saying, "Man, there is nothing like goin' to sleep to music and then wakin' up to music."

"No shit," one of his buddies agreed, glancing around, pushing the hair out of his eyes and then cracking his knuckles, "this is like Mass on Sunday morning."

"I'm saved! We've all been saved! I guess it's time to take Communion," the last one hollered to the crowd, pulling a baggie of weed from his pants pocket.

Those close by laughed with him as we ambled along, then I inquired, "I noticed the Oregon plates on the buses this morning. Didn't you say you were from Oakland?"

"That's where I grew up. Darren and Teresa live in Salem."

"And their friends in the other bus? Are they from Salem?"

"Steve and Sandy live in Springfield. Darren and Steve were college buddies at Cal Berkeley. They both teach."

"That's cool. Both of them look to be in their 30s."

"So, Teresa is four-years older than me, and Darren is three-years older than her. He's like thirty-one."

"And what level do they teach, what kind of classes?"

"Darren is a professor at Willamette University, he teaches history and Steve is at the University of Oregon. He's a year older than Darren, he teaches poli-sci. They both have their PhD's but don't have tenure yet."

"And, lemme guess, you're going to teach too. I mean you told me yesterday that you graduated with an English Lit degree, right, so, have you gotten your certificate?"

"I have," she replied with a sprite grin. "I've done all my student teaching but I decided to take time off. I'm living with Teresa and Darren. This is like our summer vacation. We actually left Salem two weeks ago. Camped at Mt. Hood and then Spirit Lake at Mount Saint Helens. It's been fun, but — this is the best."

When she said that she looked at me and beamed brightly with a smile so warm. *Did she just send a signal?*

Someone was walking in a new town and finding something special, And it's all's going to be okay, Bright feathers and wings, Fairy tales and angels dancing, Green flowers, Tapestries, What can be seen.

We came to find ourselves at the top of the tree line, before us was the same mossy log on the ground from the day before, now soaked with moisture. Gazing out over the crowd, the smoke from campfires rose in a lazy upward dance with a mashed potato sky. The words of Dino Valenti swirled around a congress of heads and freaks below us as the miracle of wonder touched our souls.

"This is so incredibly beautiful, even with the rain."

"Absolutely. It's a beautiful sight, and his voice is so perfect. What a wonderful time, to be here, right now."

"Can I read some of your writing?" Allison asked, unassumingly.

She caught me off guard, but I automatically took off my backpack and dug out the notebook I'd been using.

"Okay, sure, why not. But you have to understand that these are mostly just notes that I'll work from once I do the final. It's kinda like fragments and tangents."

"I get it, and I don't have my red pen. I won't grade it," she said with a chuckle as I handed the notebook to her.

While I listened to Dino sing his songs, Allison read through my notes, marked up drafts and thoughts. She silently turned over pages, sometimes nodding to herself, other times chuckling under her breath.

"Okay everybody! Let's give a big hand to Dino Valenti! Let's hear it everyone. Come on!" Buddha hollered. "That's right! That's right! Now we've got a special guest who's come from British Columbia today to speak with us, let's give a warm welcome to Chief Dan George! Alright! Chief Dan George everybody!"

Walking out from backstage was the same man we'd seen earlier but now he had on a black top hat with feathers sticking up behind it and was wearing a long blue woolen coat. The crowd erupted in cheers, the Natives in the crowd all began to do war whoops and calls as they danced their traditional dances in circles. At the microphone he bowed with his hands in prayer, the crowd fell silent, he began to speak with a deep soothing voice.

"My heart soars like a hawk to be here with you today. I want to thank Mr. Chambless and Mr. Noe for donating their profits to us and thank all the volunteers who helped make this festival happen. Thank you. My people and our Nation thank you with all our hearts," he said graciously. He bowed again and continued, "Oh, Great Father, give us back the wisdom of the Great Chief's. Let us contend with the times of our world. Let us again live in happiness. All of us together with our environment. As one, we will soar!"

The entire place roared with human thunder as the Chief pounded his Eagle-headed walking stick on the stage as he gazed out over the crowd with a benevolent smile.

"At this time, I would like to offer a chant to help make the clouds part and for the warmth of the sun to shine down upon us," he said, as the crowd grew silent.

"Oh, Great Spirit," he began, "we need the rain to water our crops when the summer sun has dried out the Earth." He dramatically hit the stage floor with his stick twice, then continued,

"We need the rain to fill our rivers and streams to fulfill our salmon. But today, on this sacred day of celebration, Oh Great Spirit," he said, pounding the stage again with his eagled walking stick, looking upward. "We need the warmth of the sun to dry our tired feet, we need the summer sun to return for all these beautiful people, Together, we shall chant, Sun! Sun! Sun! No rain! Sun! Sun! Sun!"

Instantly, everyone joined in, their voices loud and clear and for a brief moment the sun broke through the clouds. Chief George smiled and bowed once more to the crowd with his hands in prayer as Buddha walked back to center stage hollering, "Sun! Sun! Sun!"

"It worked! It's a miracle! Thank you, Chief! Chief Dan George, everybody!" he yelled as the ragtag community of heads, freaks and Natives all savored the experience, basking in the wisdom of his heartfelt words and their meaning in a glorious moment under the all to fleeting summer sunshine.

"How about that! Next up," Buddha said, "we're gonna have a real treat. Let's hear it for The Youngbloods, let's hear it!"

"Oh, man," Allison said, slapping the notebook down on her thigh. "My sister wants to see these guys! She loves The Youngblood's! I gotta get back and babysit."

"Right. I need to do my job and get you to your duty."

"I have to go."

"I'll go."

"No, no. You need to stay and work on your article, which is good. I can tell you have a very distinctive style and voice. From the small amount I read, I like it. You're gonna get a passing grade, so far."

She handed me the notebook and started to walk away. "No, wait! I'll walk back with you. I've got all day and, well, I'd very much rather spend it with you. If you don't mind."

"Really," she said, turning around and smiling wide.

"Absolutely!"

Off we went scrambling down the hill, around and in between all the muddy clothes and shoes, dogs, campfire smoke, pot smoke, lines for food, people, hippies, nomads, plus more at the SaniKans, while above it all, the feeling of transformation overtook our consciousness.

As I followed Allison, my internal excitement meter clanged. A sensorium of culture and counterculture surrounded us in sharp relief. I could feel a palpable balance between the two, like the line between the horizon and the sky, the break at the water's edge and the thin, hardly seen line between the yin and the yang.

Were these people writing the unwritten?

The festival was like a country within the county, a nation of freaks and intellectuals, stoned out hipsters and a wise old Indian Chief. A mosaic of the new way. Passports unneeded, the only thing called for was a state of mind within a state of sublime in a land of the all-new deal. Refinement? No, not necessarily. We were surrounded by nature in a field of awakened itinerant youth, all the same, all equal. *Had these travelers invented a new beginning? Is the real truth to be discovered here? Was a new world unfolding in front of our eyes? I think it was.* Like-minded souls, searching and finding inclusion right here in the wet woods, a big wide-open moment of assembled freedoms.

“Hello, Sky River! It’s great to be here today! This one’s off our first album; it’s called *Grizzly Bear!* Time to dance!” The bass player said into the mic as the sun came out again. The guitar player picked the intro and the song took off —

He woke up in the morning only to find that his girlfriend had left him, She was gone to Frisco to dance, Then lamented how he used to dance with her, But he can’t since she’d left him, gone.

At the water pump a crowd had built, people with empty bottles and various water containers. A woman with dark hair and glasses, blue jeans in muddy farm boots was saying something to them.

“We’ve never ran out of water like this. I just sent someone to the city of Sultan to see if they can get their water truck up here as soon as possible. So, hold on, enjoy the music.”

“Wow! They’re out of water,” I remarked. “That could be a problem.”

“No kidding. Good thing we’ve got a huge tank full. Ninety-gallons, Darren told me once. He filled it when we got here.”

"Oh, nice. You know, I saw you guys when I got to town on Friday. You were both parked at the Chevron station."

"You did?"

"Yep, I did!"

"What'd you think when you saw us?"

"Well, let's see. I think I remember saying to myself something like, 'Looks like the hippies are here . . . and I wondered what the long poles on top of your bus were for.'"

"Cool."

12:38 pm

At the campground, Teresa was standing outside the bus, holding her daughter on her hip and waving, profusely, "Hurry up! My favorite band's playing! C'mon, hurry!"

"I know. I know you love them. I'm reporting for duty!"

Darren stepped down the stairs of the bus holding the hand of their son who was walking, taking tiny, yet big steps. "What's going on over there? Teresa's been chopping at the bit and ready to go for the last half-hour."

"I saw some other kids up there," Allison offered.

"Oh, no. Not my kids. The music is too loud for their ears, and besides, I wanna have some fun too, you know."

She gently placed her daughter in Allison's hands, then said, "So, Cliff, this is Lydia, and that," she added, tilting her head towards Darren, "is Bodhi."

"Hi Lydia. Hi Bodhi. I'm Cliff, Allison's friend."

She cowered when I stepped towards her but Bohdi walked right over to me, reached out and touched my pant leg. "Hey buddy. You're a good-looking guy."

"Go ahead, you can pick him up and hold him if you'd like," Darren offered, just as a bank of clouds blotted out the sun. "Any friend of Allison's is a friend of ours. Don't worry, go ahead, we trust you."

I looked at Teresa for approval and she nodded, then glanced at Allison and she was smiling, brightly. So, I picked up Bohdi and held him on my hip, grinning.

“Okay, we’re off,” Teresa said. As they were leaving, she turned around and offered, “Cliff, you should come to dinner tonight. We’re doing a big spaghetti feed.”

I looked over to Allison, she was nodding. “Yes, I’d like that very much. Thank you!” I turned back to Allison and she tilted her head at the doorway and, we got on the bus.

Inside, Allison went straight to the dinette and sat down with Lydia and started bouncing her on her knee. I sat across from her with Bodhi. Looking around I was able to take in much more than in the morning. Large refrigerator with a yin and yang symbol on its door, next to it a counter and sink. Two sets of bunk beds in the back against the side walls, cupboards and shelving ran along the roof line with a horizontal finished wood edge to stop things from falling. A doored off room that I guessed was a bathroom, small wood heater with a brick surround and kindling, hooks with clothes hanging and lots of books. It had that same sweet smell I’d been noticing for days.

"It took Darren a couple years of weekends to build it."

"He did an excellent job, and um, what's that aroma?"

"Patchouli. It's an essential oil that's extracted from the patchouli plant. Don't you just love it? I sure do."

"I do. I've been noticing it quite a bit this weekend."

"Oh yeah, us earthy folks like that kind of thing," Allison said. Then she looked down at Lydia and sniffed. "I think somebody just pooped their diaper. I don't think Cliff wants to stick around for this. Good thing there's plenty of patchouli in this place."

"Oh, I don't mind. That's all part of the deal, right?"

"No, no. You need to get back up to the show and work on your article. What was it you said yesterday, 'Get a feel for things.' We'll be fine."

"You're sure? Because I'm happy to stay. I really like this."

Lydia started squirming on her lap. "Believe me, it's alright. You need to work and besides, I'll see you at dinner time," she added with a big bright beautiful smile. I set Bodhi down on the floor, he went straight to a bunk bed and pulled himself up into it.

"Okay," I said, standing up. "You think you might come up in a while? Maybe catch some music?"

"That all depends on my sister. She likes to dance and party, just like the rest of us. She taught me everything."

"Oh, she did? My big brother didn't teach me anything." I wanted to give her a kiss or a hug but with Lydia in her arms. *I think I'll hold off.*

"Alright, I'll look for you at the festival but if I don't see you then I'll see you at dinner. I'll be here for sure. See you soon." I raised my hand in good-bye and smiled.

On my way out I took notice of some books on the sofa. *Green Eggs and Ham*, *Dr. Suess's Sleep Book* and beside them, *The Teachings of Don Juan* and *Sometimes a Great Notion.* It was an eclectic display.

Walking away I smiled. A wonderful feeling of deep affection flooded over me just as a pregnant charcoal cloud gave birth to a torrential rain child. It screamed a river of life from the sky, the drops dancing a merry melody on the pavement. They fell in a musical rhythm that beat upon every leaf on every alder tree. It rained a downbeat tom-tom, it played a flourish of cascading notes that spilled into streams and waterways, soaking broad leaf lupine and columbine, drenching every soul with lifegiving water.

At the ticket booth I saw Roger and held up a soggy piece of pink paper up for him to see as I approached.

"How's it going?" I asked, walking by. He nodded back and raised his hand. "Goin' good. How you doin'?"

"Never better!" As I climbed the short hill the music got louder and the Youngbloods were playing an upbeat, feel-good song. The singers voice fresh and clear. Then magically, the sky cleared and bright and warm wonderful sunshine shone down from a clearing sky.

Mama's in the kitchen while Daddy's in another room, And someone else was waiting on his girlfriend, Euphoria, But then another man showed up hiding under the counter who had a good job, Yet that didn't matter because he was head over heels in love with his gal, His one and only true love, His very own Euphoria.

To my great jaw dropping surprise and astonishment, a fellow, black with mud from head to toe, walked right by me. *What on earth?* His clothes were completely covered in slimy mud. His white teeth standing out.

"Hey! Mud Man!" somebody shouted. "Headed to the pond?"

The guy raised a blackened arm into the air and continued. Down in front but off to the side of the stage a giant mud pit was filled with a dozen or more happy, muddy people. One guy came running down the hill, slipping and sliding, and launched himself forward, taking a dive onto the mud and then slid head first into a pool of black spring water and earth. Right behind him a woman in a white blouse did the same.

Holy shit, look at this! What a sight! I instantly ripped off my pack, got out my pen and notebook, got down on my haunches and started writing, fast.

The theme of day-two was great barrelhouse rock and mud. With the Youngbloods for a musical backdrop and the overnight rainfall providing a mud pit as big as an Olympic sized pool the Sky River Rock Festival transformed itself into a gigantic mud bath for dozens of hippies and freaks. The world's biggest Slip-n-Slide Mud Ride was free for anyone bold enough to act like a kid again. Playing the hours away in slippery, slimy black ooze without a care in the world under the sun.

When the song ended the bass player stepped up to the microphone and said, "Looks like you folks are havin' way too much fun down there. Maybe I'll join you a while. Here's one that'll fit right in. I think you'll like it."

Daddy taught his son all about booze and beer, But wine was the best, Need to drink it every day and stay drunk all the time, Drinking that good old sparkly wine.

Then another one came running down the slippery slope and threw himself forward, sliding head first into the mud pit. Over and over, one after another. All of them smiling, showing bright white teeth against black muddy faces, like piglets in hog gravy. I'd never seen so many people as dirty and happy before in my life. Mud, mud, and more mud. Then

Mud Man was back, in sopping wet clothes, but clean. He'd obviously had a dip in the pond and returned to cheer on his fellow Mud People, throwing and pumping his fist in the air in victorious triumph.

With sonorous music and the thick dank aroma of weed aloft they both coagulated with the mud people making for a sight that I'm sure would be remembered. Glancing around I saw Darren and Teresa dancing away with Steve and Sandy and then spied that same group from earlier, with the dapper cowboy and the orange robed dark-bearded fellow. A few more people had joined them. A tall blonde woman wearing a long red schall was drinking from a white cup and a cooler was on the ground next to them. They were intriguing to me, so I casually inched my way over nearer to them as Buddha took the microphone.

"Let's hear it for the Youngbloods! Come on! Clap people! You too, Mud People! Let's give them a big hand! Okay, okay everybody, so tomorrow we're working on something that might just blow your mind away. Right off the face of the earth!"

"What?"

"Tell us!"

"You said the same thing about The Beatles yesterday!"

"Who? What's happening tomorrow?!?"

"Nope, I can't tell you yet, maybe in a awhile. But if it happens it's gonna be bigger than big. So huge it'll be far-out! Okay so now, next up we've got The James Cotton Blues Band and they're gonna be up here in a few minutes to play you all some powerful blues but while they set up, I've got some announcements to make. Alright, so everybody listen up! Ma Kahuna, the kind owner of this beautiful farm has arranged with the city of Sultan for them to bring out their water truck since her well has gone dry and the natural spring is now filled with mud. We don't know exactly when the truck will be here but Sultan has assured Ma that the truck will be here sometime today. Then all you Mud People can take a bath! Hahaha! But really, I hear there's a pond up the hill that you can all use to clean off. Also, Ma needs you all to know that if you want to have a campfire that's okay, but to only use the dead limbs and sticks you find out in the woods on the ground. You got that! Good!"

While Buddha did his thing, I slowly worked my way nearer to the dapper cowboy gang. They had an intellectual hippie vibe to them that was attracting. I found myself being drawn to their conversations and lingered inconspicuously nearby.

"So, Tom," the orange dressed fellow said, "are you going to take a muddy dive into the pit? Take the big slide?"

"Not for me," dapper guy replied. "My momma may have called me Tommy Rotten, but there's no way I'm doing that. Just because we're here to challenge society that doesn't mean I'm going to do it the dirty way," he said, making a sweeping arm movement, taking in the surroundings. Just then a couple of Mud People walked by, headed uphill to the pond. Once they were out of range, dapper guy offered, "I guess some folks just require more understanding than others." Everyone in his group chuckled and then he added, "They apparently know that LSD will turn you into a fun-loving fiend. Just like us!" His whole group was laughing wildly at his observations when he reached down and opened the cooler. He pulled the tab off a can of Pepsi, and then took a big gulp.

"Since we are self-exiled here for the weekend, I say we all get lost in the robust charm of the moment."

"Okay everybody!" Buddha hollered, "it's time for the James Cotton Blues Band! Give 'em a hand everyone!"

"How's everybody doin' out there?!" Cotton asked. He had an engaging look on his face with a get after it grin. A tray of harmonicas was on a stool next to him, he picked up a silver one then grabbed hold of the microphone stand, jerked the mic out of it and called, "Oowee! We all got some Mississippi Mud back home but nothin' like this," he observed, motioning to the pit and its people. They cheered back and then Cotton turned back to his band, a guitarist, bass player, drummer and a fellow on the piano. He counted off a song and they broke into a rockin' blues number that got everyone on their feet, screaming and dancing along.

Some man didn't care if the world fell apart, Because he was so in love with his woman, Her love burned for him too, Like they were both ablaze and yet, She still needed to take it slow.

He brought the microphone and harp up to his mouth and it exploded with clear, clean notes. His body bending and moving around the stage, the band tight and loud. The tone of every note he blew was precise and forceful and his band thumped out a deep rhythm. Cotton was a man in his prime, lean and muscular, his movements like a cat on the prowl. The crowd was with him, cheering him on, moving, swaying, hollering, urging him while he vamped to the throng when a black woman appeared at the side of the stage. Dressed in a tight white dress with pearls around her neck, she danced a sultry dance, moving her hips slow, while clapping her hands. Cotton sauntered over to her as he wailed away. Talk about sexy, it oozed out from both of them, and the band.

2:49 pm

A dark yet clairvoyant rain cloud dodged past the tribal music dancers, holding its fruits of labor for farther up the valley. Soon it would rain a whirlwind upon all who dared to scoff at the wild frivolities of the Now Generation. To the enlightened, the rain signaled a clean, fresh path, the trail to knowledge and awareness, each drop a note, each liquid pearl a gift. It washed away the years of social mores that could no longer chain down the dynasty youth who stomped in writhing rhythms of freeness and spirit. Who couldn't be held down by the open feeling that cascaded in a flood of joyful tears for a new world, a new way, a new kind of expression. Turning back from the barbaric past, charting a new course to sail upon fresh waters.

An hour later, rumbling and diesel exhaust held attention over the howling harp of James Cotton. Turning around I saw a black and gray tanker truck with white letters, City of Sultan, on its door. It pulled up in front of Ma Kahuna's roughhewn cottage close to the well. A man hopped out of the cab glancing around at all the happy bedlam with a bewildered look on his face, a set of red suspenders holding up a pair of denim jeans. A gaggle of thirsty people instantly gathered around him and his truck holding canteens, empty glass bottles and plastic milk jugs that needed filling. I wandered over to them to check out the situation.

"Hold on, hold on! Let's try and form some kind of a line, people," the city worker said. The vertical white letters L-O-U-I-E were on his suspenders. He unfurled a length of water hose and turned a valve, "Okay, folks, step right up and get yourselves some Lake 16 water, it's the best darn water in this here county."

"Thanks mister."

"Thank you, sir."

"Looks like most of you could use a bath," Louie remarked, shaking his head as he filled the containers. But then he looked over at the stage and grinned.

The next time everything wouldn't be the same, Everything isn't shiny jewels or gold, Someone had fabricated and cheated, So somebody new has taken his woman's place on her pedestal.

"Thank you, Sky River!" Cotton said waving good-bye. "It's been great! Thank you! Ya'll gotta do this again!"

"The James Cotton Blues Band!" Buddha hollered.

Day two also brought the legendary James Cotton Blues Band who tore the place apart. Cotton's harmonica playing exploded across the stage and got everyone on their feet. His tight band thumped a deep beat while

Cotton prowled the stage like a hungry tiger and his voice growled like thunder —

"Let's hear it for James Cotton everybody and let's give a big hand to the city for bringing their water truck to our rescue. Thank you, Sultan!" Buddha cried out to the crowd as cheers came up from the mass of muddy humanity.

"Next, we've got folk artist Mark Spoelstra who is gonna come out and sing for us. Where's Mark?" Buddha said. He turned towards the side of the stage and a red-headed thin man with a thick goatee walked out with a 12-string guitar carrying a stool. At the microphone he sat down, gazed out over the crowd and asked, "How's everybody doin' out there? I heard you had a long night last night. Plenty of sky water then, right?" he said to laughs. "Looks like we got some real water now thanks to the city! So, here's one from my last release, a very appropriate tune." He picked the intro, then started singing.

A protest about how important life is and not to be wasted on the crime of the war, How worried his mind was because of all the lying in our country, One must live.

His voice filled the natural amphitheater, strong and clear, it bounced off the forest and circled around with the breeze. After a good number of songs, I made my way back over to where the dapper cowboy gang was holding court, I couldn't help but listen to their lively back and forth banter.

"Did you know that the common cockroach has been living on this planet for millions of years? Those roaches are tough little mothers," dapper guy observed. He had a touch of the south in his voice.

"Well, they're not as tough as the ones in your Valient's ashtray!" the guy in the orange smock replied.

"Aren't you a saucy peach," the cowboy replied. "Especially in that robe you've got on. Where'd you get that?"

The fellow in the orange tunic grinned and took a second while everyone in the group waited with anticipation.

"It doesn't matter where I got it. What matters is I'm challenging society and we are not going away, no matter what kind or what color of clothes we choose."

"Yeah, well," the dapper one replied, "I'm gonna go Baptize some trees. But before I go, did you know that human beings were created by water as a device to transport itself from one place to another?" he said with the look of fun and frivolity on his face. And again, everyone burst out laughing, including me. The fellow had an air about him that triggered a remarkable inner goofiness in me, and others apparently.

Everyone should be in the jailhouse, We all wish that those in DC were all in the jailhouse for the war and the draft.

"Let's hear it for Mark Spoelstra! Mark Spoelstra everyone!" Buddha cried out again to the now thirst satisfied crowd. "And while you're at it lets give a big cheer to the water guy over there manning the truck!"

When Louie heard that he hopped up on the back of his tanker smiling wide, then doffed his newsboy hat, bowing.

Folk artist Mark Spoelstra was a joy. Both he and Cotton were worth more than the price of admission. The City of Sultan's water truck arrived only a few hours after the land-owners well had gone dry. Festival goers cheered "Louie," the city employee who graciously took the time to come out on Labor Day weekend —

"Next up we're gonna bring out the San Francisco Mime Troupe Marching Band! They all drove up here from the Bay Area so let's give them a big hand!"

Out from the side of the stage paraded a long line of Mardi Gras like revelers, a rag-tag group dressed in all manner of patchwork cloaks, jester hats, jerkins and tights, most with instruments, others with medieval walking sticks, men and women, young and old. One guy beat a big bass drum that had a gorilla face drawn on it, behind him a snare drum, then plastic horns, tin penny whistles, tambourines, kazoos, a trumpet, clarinet, and all of them tootling away doing, *When the Saints Go Marching In.* Those without instruments were singing at the top of their lungs.

Like circus clowns they marched out-of-sync, singing, playing, bending over then straightening up, carrying on as if they were having the time of their lives, it was commedia dell'arte. Confusion and chaos took over the stage and then, and then, they abruptly stopped and started gazing around like they were lost, looking up and down, left and right, and ka-boom! They went into, *Yankee Doodle Dandy*. More banging and wild clarinet playing, the trumpet blew loud and the crowd howled with laughter and cheered with side aches. Back and forth they marched in disarray and sang, bumping into each other, stopping and bowing to their crazily dressed companions when they did.

Next, two jugglers appeared tossing bowling pins to each other between the players causing as much havoc as they could. The colorful display brought happiness and joy to the crowd, every face lit up with cheer and jubilation. And then, and then, they all stopped again and glanced around, the crowd fell silent and, *The Star-Spangled Banner* began. When the singers got to, *the rocket's red glare*, some would moan and groan. At, *bombs bursting in air*, they all stopped and screamed to the heavens. Howls of laughter erupted. Some of the women, like majorettes, carried painted signs with fragmented letters. As the band played on the majorettes lined up at the front of the stage and put their signs together forming, GET OUT OF VIETNAM, and the crowd went bonkers with cheers and clenched fists striking the air.

With that, they went into, *The Battle Hymn of the Republic.* The majorettes led them off stage while playing but then they reappeared at the side entrance and began marching through the crowd. Singing the somber ode, they weaved their way back and forth, bypassing the mud pit, and then made one final giant circle, went through the side stage gate and it was over.

5:23 pm

It didn't take long to walk to the campground. Tablecloths laid, plates and cutlery placed and folding chairs set out. Teresa and Allison were busy arranging plastic flowers in vases as I approached. Bodhi and Lydia were sitting on a blanket on top of a tarp on the ground playing with tinker toys and Steve's wife sat quietly, looking demur, drinking wine. Darren and Steve were in the middle of a lively conversation.

". . . because we cannot continue treating the natural world as if it's separate from ourselves. The human race, us, everyone, the fascists, the cops, the union man, the white collared suits, we all have to realize that we are *all* part of the environment. We are one! The population is inclusive with the natural world; it's not two separate things and we need to start taking care of it. No more polluting."

"And I agree, wholeheartedly," Darren replied, sitting with his legs crossed in a folding chair, a glass of wine in his hand. "But after what Daley did in Chicago a few days ago and since that asshole killed our candidate, the bulk of this county isn't gonna put Humphrey and Muskie in the White House to help with the environment. I mean, I'll vote for them, but I don't think they've got a chance. The voting public I believe thinks Humphrey's a wimpy suck up."

"Yeah, I get all that," Steve replied, "but Daley and the Republicans wants a police state. They want us violent because then they get what they want. And that's to beat on us and have a reason to put us behind bars, to control us. I think Hoffman and Rubin were out for fame when they invented their so-called *Festival of Life* thing to get everyone to go to Chicago. Well, Daley, he didn't dig on that because nothing happens in Chicago without his approval, he had his goons beat everyone up. I liked Rubin when he was organizing protests at Berkeley but after this, I'm not so sure about him. I think Hoffman and him were partly to blame for getting everyone to go there, that was their risk, that they took. I think they're just a couple of hustlers, out to become famous and make a buck. In a few more years they'll probably be washed up parodies of themselves."

"Oh, I have absolutely no doubt about that. The police and the government want total control. Just like the cops that shut down the Haight. They couldn't control it so they used all the runaway kids for an excuse with daily sweeps carding suspect juveniles and tossing them in their paddy wagons if they were underage. Plus, they set up all those big orange spot lights that burned all night long so it looked like a prison yard and then turned Haight Street into a one-way only. Plus, what was really ridiculous was when they started busting kids for doing chalk art on the sidewalks. They handled everything so poorly. So much for the land of the free."

"Oh, that is so right on, and the other thing that is driving me right now is the fact that our natural world is not sustainable. I want to do something for it, and I refuse to be some replaceable bolt in the wheel of consumer life. I wanna do something from the ground up and make a difference. You know, leave the world a better place than when we were here. We need to focus on the long haul and stop being a throw away society. Can ya' dig it? We need, the world needs, to start reprocessing all those aluminum beer and pop cans, glass, and paper too. If we don't start reusing every product we can, then there's just not going to be that many tomorrows. We need to do it for the children, all the children," he said, motioning at Darren and Teresa's two kids playing on the blanket.

"The children of this country are the future there's no doubt about that. And they all need access to an affordable education. There's no reason why every college can't be free like we had it at Cal, public schools through high school are free for the students and that should be extended to the college level, at every institution."

"You bet!" Steve exclaimed. "But what most people don't understand is that the dull mind is what the government wants, because then, they can hold power over us. So, the government will fight against free college, they mean to keep the people down. We are the ones who have to make real fundamental change happen in this country. But everyone has to understand that change only happens one person at a time. All those people out there," Steve said, gesturing, "have to change in a positive, loving way, and if everyone did that then the world would be a better place and this counterproductive malarkey would end. Not to mention that the corruption in the upper crust of this country must stop before it gets out of hand. All those white-collar criminals need to be prosecuted just like every other common law breaker."

Then Buddha came over the PA system. "Okay everyone, next up we've got H.P. Lovecraft! All the way from Chicago! Let's hear it for H.P. Lovecraft!"

"Good afternoon, Sky River! Good to be here! This first one's titled *The White Ship*. We hope you like it."

The ship has left everyone behind, Floating on visions, Below a shrouded moon and burning tides.

Just then Allison caught a glimpse of me from the corner of her eye. She turned and smiled a dreamy smile and walked straight at me and hugged me, saying, "Thanks for coming. I'm really glad you're here. Did you get any —"

"There's the man of the hour," Darren said, standing up.

“This must be Cliff,” Steve said, standing, reaching out to shake hands. “This is my wife, Sandy. Good to meet you.”

“Nice meeting you too,” I said to both of them, shaking their hands. “So, Teresa, this all looks wonderful. Thank you for inviting me,” I said to her across the table.

She grinned, walked over to me and remarked, “Thanks for coming. What did you think of The Youngbloods?”

“They were great. Liked ‘em a lot.”

“They’re my favorite. I just love Jesse Colin Young’s voice.” She handed me a glass then filled it with Almaden red wine.

“And what about that marching band. They were a kick.”

“I wouldn’t know,” Allison said, grabbing my hand and pulling me towards the bus and leading us inside. She sat me down on the sofa and looked into my eyes.

“What do you think of my world,” she said, tilting her head towards her family outside.

"I like 'em," I replied, taking a sip of wine. "They seem like intelligent up to date people that care. Just like you."

"Oh, I love my big sister, she taught me everything."

"You mentioned that earlier. So, you didn't come back up to the show. I was looking for you, hoping I'd see you. Even with all the rain and mud it was great."

"I decided to stay and help Teresa with the kids and dinner. Are you going to be here tomorrow?"

"Absolutely."

"Oh, good, I want you all to myself. Did you get high today?"

"No."

"Okay, but if Steve or Darren start rolling joints after dinner just take a little puff. The weed they have is super strong and we don't need you wandering off and falling asleep in the woods?" She said with her cute little pixie smile.

I nodded at her in approval then quietly answered, “Alright.”

“I want you to enjoy yourself, it’s just that, they like to smoke a lot of pot after dinner and socialize. Let’s go back outside.” She stood up but then stopped, “They’re anti-cigarettes too so, um, try not to lite one up.”

“Funny you mentioned that because, I didn’t bring them today.”

“Thats-a-good. I can see you’re learning. Growing. Nice. Let’s go back out and sit with everyone.”

The empty shoreline, A deserted beach, But strong winds blow, The White Ship to its home.

“Daley’s the one who should’ve been beaten, thrown in a paddy wagon and tossed in jail like the bum he is. And the mere fact that our boys are getting drafted at 18 and not having the right to vote, when they’re over fighting a war over in far-away Vietnam and dying,” Steve said, his eyes on fire, “well, that, that’s criminal.”

“I’m pretty sure Daley was leaking to reporters that there’d been threats of assassination against himself, well, that's pure baloney. He made the claim for an excuse to beat on those kids, just because he didn't like them staying in his stupid little park. Plus, he said that they were gonna spike Chicago's water system with LSD. I mean, c'mon, really?"

Darren turned to me as I was sitting down and said, "Cliff, Allison tells me you work for a newspaper. What do you think about all this democratic convention brouhaha?"

I took a bigger sip of wine, then said, "I think that Mayor Daley was in the wrong, but I just report what happens. My editor would never let me do an opinion piece. Well, not yet anyway. But I do cover local politics."

"Oh, you cover politics. So, who are you going to vote for this fall?" Steve asked.

Uh-oh, here we go, the fats in the fire now. "I'll be voting the Democratic ticket."

"Good."

"However, I do try my best to be non-biased in all of my reporting."

I glanced over to Allison; she shrugged her shoulders.

Gathering my thoughts I continued. “But when I declared journalism as my major my dad told me that I probably shouldn’t vote so that I’d be biased free and independent in my reporting. But like most of young America today, I didn’t listen. I think it’s incredibly important to vote in all elections.”

The table was quiet for a bit until Teresa spoke up. “Good for you, we need independent reporters in the world. That’s why we have the Fairness Doctrine. Isn’t that right, Darren?” she said, glancing at her husband and then at me, saving my bacon.

“Yes, honey that’s true, you’re right. But you must have an opinion,” he said, looking at me again. “If your editor let you write an op-ed column in the Sunday paper, what would you say? What topic would you choose?”

I took a gulp of wine, then answered, “Oh, I’m sure old man Corson would never entertain the thought. For the last year I’ve been relegated to attending city council meetings. I pretty much just listen and then report what went on. I’m not a hard news guy and somewhat shy. But if he did let me write an opinion piece, I’d write about Vietnam and, oh, this uprising spirit of youth,” I said, gesturing towards the festival.

"And let's see, I think I'd write about the false prophecy of Richard Nixon, he's a scoundrel and not to be trusted. I mean, him flashing the peace sign at their convention was so phony I thought, completely fake. But then what politician can be trusted? Well, Bobby Kennedy. I think he would have been a great president. I liked his brother a lot, but the rest of these old white dullards in suits who sit behind desks and start wars but don't fight in them and don't allow their sons to fight in them because they know war's wrong, is wrong. And *that,* to me, is totally disgusting."

"Good answer," Teresa quickly said, saving me once again. "Enough with the politics. It's dinnertime!"

Sandy stood up and followed her and Allison into the green bus then Teresa came back out with a large stainless-steel bowl full of spaghetti and noodles. Sandy carried another bowl of salad and Allison had loaves of French bread. They set them down on the tables while Darren pulled two highchairs from the storage area under his bus.

"What can I do?" I asked, watching all the commotion.

“Just sit and look pretty,” Allison replied with her dreamy smile. “Right there, next to me,” she said, pointing at a folding chair. I grinned at her and winked.

Once seated, I asked, “That MC, Buddha guy, he mentioned something big for tomorrow. Any ideas on that?”

The whole table turned their heads at me and then Sandy spoke up, “I think he talks ways too much and is too repetitive. Why should we believe him when he said that The Beatles might show up. What a line of crap that was. I heard he’s a bouncer at some bar in San Francisco, and a deejay, so I would guess that if there is a surprise band that shows up it would be another group from down there. Maybe Quicksilver Messenger Service. That is, even if he’s telling the truth. And I doubt it. He was the wrong choice to MC.”

“Oh, but if he’s right,” Teresa added, “I would love to see Gracie Slick show up with the Airplane or maybe it’s Janis and Big Brother. That would be cool.”

Then Steve raised his glass and said, “Here’s to The Sky River Rock Festival and Lighter Than Air Fair!”

XII

Day Three

Glorious sunshine soaked the valley. Enlightened by the sunrise, the Cascades came alive, their rugged luminescence glistening in golden rays from the living sun. The majesty of crags and peaks resounding grace and adventure, the broad narrative of its range drawn out along the eastern horizon.

Upriver, the ancients lived in these mountains. They fished the salmon runs, hunted deer and elk, gathered roots and berries, their canoes plied the Skykomish River. The Indigenous built longhouses in villages along the water where they'd host gift-giving potlaches to socialize intertribal relationships. Drank from and bathed in the clear cool river that nourished their families while the spirit world took care of and looked over them.

Today's festival of gathering tribes is now played out with music and the freedom to venture at will. Partake in the substance of plant-based mind awareness with the expression of sharing, understanding, and love.

I stopped writing and thought, *oh man, I can't wait to see Allison* — when someone outside made a, "Yelp." I looked at my watch, it was 6:51. Peeking through the drapes I saw two fellows cramming a rolled-up section of rug into the trunk of a car and speeding off. *Did they just cut-up some carpet, steal it, and take off?* I looked down at the green and yellow shag carpeting in my room. *Geez, it's not that nice.*

After a long hot shower, I put on my last clean T-shirt and pair of socks, I guess I didn't pack enough since I still had one more day. My boots were a muddy mess so I took some time to clean them and was ready.

Outside, a sheriff's car was parked at the office. *Bonnie must already know about the theft.* In the café, the room was rife with talk and speculation, the pleasing aroma of bacon fat and fresh coffee in the air.

"What a bunch of idiots, they probably didn't think that we always double check our guests license plates with the numbers they write down at check in," Don said from his kitchen station, flipping pancakes. "They'll get caught. Guess I'll be calling my insurance guy."

"What would a couple of stupid hippies want with your carpet?"

"That's what I've been asking myself all morning, Sam."

"Gosh, you're hangin' tough for the long haul, aren't you?"

I recognized the voice. It was Doreen, turning my cup over and filling it with fresh steaming coffee.

"What'll it be, Sugar," she asked, her hair still a teased mess.

"How about a tall stack of flapjacks and a side of bacon?"

"Okay Hun."

"Last day for the rock show," Don offered, setting two plates up on the counter under the heat lamps. Just then the sheriff's car zoomed off, lights flashing. Bonnie came rushing into the café, flustered.

"Deputy Briggs had an emergency and needed to go," she imparted to the room, "but he left me his card to give to anyone who saw something this morning on the carpet theft." She looked around the cafe for a response. "If anyone saw something he wants them to call." Nobody did or said anything so I raised my hand.

"I saw them, a couple of Heads, um, longhairs, two of 'em."

"Okay, good, thank you," Bonnie said walking over to my table. She held out his card for me to take then said to everyone, "He told me that the Ben Howard Road is only going to be one-way today. From Sultan to Monroe. There's too much traffic, they're all parking in or on the side of the road, it's a huge problem."

"Okay, thanks," I replied, looking at the deputy's card on both sides. I slipped it into my shirt pocket for another time.

"Here ya' go, Sugar," Doreen said, setting breakfast down on the table. "You gonna call the sheriff?"

"Well, probably, seeing's how I'm a reporter."

"How's the big hoedown out at Betty's going?"

"Going good, I guess." She refilled my coffee then stood and waited. "It's been, well, very disparate out there and such a contrast."

"Contrast?"

"Yes, between here in town and out there. I mean, this is quiet smalltown America and just a couple of miles away it's completely the opposite. Lots of hippies and all, you know, plenty of pot smoking and skinny dipping." She winked at me with a sly grin, bent over close, and then whispered in a silky, sexy voice.

"I think this town could use a little fun. Don't you?"

On the shuttle ride out to the festival the sun shone brightly through the bus windows and there were clearly more cars lining the road on both sides than the day before. One beat up old jalopy had the words spray painted on its side in white lettering, 'Sky River Rock Festival or Bust!'

At the empty ticket kiosk people were just coming and going as they pleased. The driver closed the door and off we went up to the campground. Once there, as I stepped from the bus Buddha started introducing the first artist.

9:38 am

"How's everybody doing out there today? Looks like we're gonna have us a dandy day! Okay, first we've got Alice Stuart Thomas. She's from Chelan over across the mountains and has played the Berkeley Folk Festival the last couple of years. Everybody! Let's give a big hand now for Alice!"

"Hello, Sky River! Good to see you today!" she said, then strummed her guitar and started singing.

Beatniks share everything in their lives without a care, When you live the life of a Beatnik, Nobody could cast a stone at them for never understanding, Because they'd never been in the home of a Beatnik.

At the campground, I looked to see if there was any movement at Allison's when the door to the green bus flew open and, out she bounded, looking like a dream come true. Blue jeans, Levi jacket, brown leather shoes that were boot-like, and her thick Raven hair flowing behind her.

Our eyes met and she waved. I did the same and hollered, "Good morning! You're up early and ready to go." As she approached, I added, "Looking wonderful today. I love that jacket."

"Oh, this thing," she blushed. Allison stepped right up close, gave me a big hug and then a peck on the cheek.

"Sleep good?"

"Very, until Lydia woke up hungry and crying, that got everyone up."

"Oh, gosh. Speaking of Lydia, and I have to say, your niece and nephew are the cutest kids on the planet, and well behaved."

"Oh, thanks. They have their grumpy times, that's for sure."

"Do you have babysitting duty again today?"

"I do, but I've got the whole morning off, they're sleeping in," she said as the shuttle bus roared off.

"Fantastic! Well, it looks like we're walking."

"Fine by me. It's good to get some exercise."

"So, um, this morning," I started, as our shoes tapped out a rhythm. "I witnessed a crime at the motel."

"You what?!"

"True story. I woke up really early and was doing some writing when I heard something outside. Then I saw these two guys loading a rolled-up carpet into the trunk of a car and speeding off."

"And?"

"And then later there was a sheriff's deputy at the office but he had an emergency and took off. But Bonnie, she's one of the owners, came in the café looking for witnesses so I said that I saw it. She gave me the deputies business card and told me to call him. I guess because they'll need a witness to identify the culprits."

"Oh, my gawd! You've had yourself a busy day already!"

“Indeed.” We walked silently for a bit, our steps beating a cadence. “I liked that last song.”

“You mean the one about the Beatniks?”

“I do. I guess I’m a one of them now. Or maybe a, what’d you call me, a proto-hippie?”

“Well, yes, one with tremendous potential. But we’re all kinda Beatniks since they laid the groundwork for us. The poets and artists of the Beat Generation were the ones who really started all of this. We grew out of them,” Allison said with a knowing voice. “The Beats showed us the way, and we followed.”

I thought about her observation and nodded approvingly then she began snapping her fingers in unison. With each snap she moved her hands up and down, saying, “Cool, daddy-o!” Snap. “Go! Go! Go!” Snap. “It was the Beats!” Snap. “The Beats!” Snap. “Thank you, Beats!” Snap. Her beautiful expression told me that she was seizing the day with her omnipresent spirit. She expounded with robust insight.

“First it was the poets and the art galleries, then the coffeehouses and the poetry readings with Ginsberg and McClure and all those guys. Kerouac would be in the crowd, urging them on, hollering, 'Go! Go!' And along in there, in that time frame, the goatees and berets showed up, then the turtlenecks and sandals and the sketch artists. I think the Beats were born out of subculture angst and a yearning for Eastern thought."

I smiled at her and said, "The Beats really were cool cats."

"Oh, undoubtedly. You see, it was the close-minded puritanical element in our government that pushed the Beats into the spotlight. When they charged Ginsberg's publisher with obscenity for selling his poem *Howl*, it made headlines and ended up having the opposite effect. They're selfish actions shined a light on Ginsberg and Ferlinghetti and all the others. Those guys kicked down the doors of the governments self-perceived immorality campaign and made the poems by him and Gary Snyder, Gregory Corso and the rest completely accessible. Through them the public learned that there was, there is, so much more to the range of human experience because of it. So now, us hippies have walked through the door they opened and carried on with that same courage to challenge society and bring our generation and our movement to the forefront."

"They really were trailblazers, weren't they? But wasn't Ferlinghetti acquitted of that charge?"

"Absolutely, the judge exonerated him. And now, the musicians of San Francisco have channeled their influence and applied rock music to Beat inspired lyrics, they've brought it to the masses, and we are carrying that torch into the future!"

"You sure seem to know a lot about them."

"I took a couple of courses on Beat literature in college plus, I grew up with them, kinda, I guess. Get this, when Ginsburg wrote *Howl,* he didn't have a title for it but he mailed a copy to Kerouac. After he read it, he wrote Ginsburg back and told him to call it *Howl.* Isn't that cool?"

"*That,* is really cool."

"Okay, well, here's another little tidbit. One day Kerouac casually mentioned to a friend that he was feeling beat down and exhausted by life and phony American optimism, and said, 'I guess one could say that we're the beat generation.' Then another friend of his heard about the comment and wrote a magazine article and titled it, *Beat.* And the term stuck."

"Geez, that's so awesome," I responded, nodding and smiling at her observation. *This woman is utterly fantastic!* As we walked by the empty kiosk I said, "The Beats were definitely groundbreakers . . . so, it looks like they're not even checking for tickets anymore."

"I guess they turned it into a free concert. I think a lot of people jumped the fencing and came in through the woods." She took me by the hand as we shambled up the hill, I turned to her and smiled, she beamed back.

Up at the farm, the place had turned into a colony of searchers and stargazers. It was absolutely jam packed with every fashion of freaks and heads. An American flag had been hung in front of the linen stage-drop facing the crowd in a fitting display of hippie love for a free and peaceful country. The festival had erupted into an extravaganza of freeform carnival performers, all of them engaged in their own counterculture movies. The entire field and up the hill was a patchwork of humanity, right up to the tree-line. Small campfires burned in the late morning sun with folks gathered around them cooking something to eat, some peeling oranges, others laying in sleeping bags out in the open, pungent pot smoke, music from the stage and the acoustic stylings of folk singer Alice Stuart Thomas.

"Gawd," Allison remarked, pointing her nose into the breeze. "I just love the smell of pot in a public place. Don't you?" She asked, looking at me with her wry roguish grin.

"You, know. Now that you mention it, I believe I do."

"I think it smells like we're winning," she pronounced, just as a familiar rumble came up the driveway. There was Louie with his city water truck again. A cheer came up from the crowd while people made way as he pulled up right where he was the day before. Jumping out he waved and took his station, people started crowding around for some fresh water.

"This whole thing is just too much. I mean —" I stopped talking and opened my rucksack, took out my writing materials and got down on my haunches. Allison smiled approvingly.

The Sky River Festival is an altruistic Mecca for people who are looking for the beauty in life that only a searcher would find in the magic of prophetic consciousness. That place in time where spiritual truth abounds and social boundaries have fallen. All *attendees discovering a setting where they can be themselves, and not be a conformist in a psychedelic mélange of color and movement. Everyone looking for true independence and finding it at Betty Nelson's Organic Raspberry Farm. There's a kinetic, palpable energy here in the backwoods and foothills of Snohomish County. A feeling of oneness and sense of joyful self-expression, a perception that, 'we can change the world' but on our own terms, in our own way. A belief in the value of sharing and that yes, we are changing the awareness of humanity. Was it fate that brought all these misfits of mischief together or was it written in the stars by the Beat Generation beforehand that paved the way and caused everyone to travel here as champions in ascendency to explore true freedoms?*

I stood back up and returned my notebook to its place. Allison had her little stone pipe and film container out. As she stuffed the bowl, she turned to me and said with a sexy little grin, "How about a morning puff?"

"Absolutely," I replied, the crush of adoration landing on my heart. S*he sure is something. Another signal perhaps?*

"Is this the same stuff we had on the first day?" I asked as she blew out the smoke then handed it to me.

"It is," she said, striking a match, "but don't hold it in, blow it out right away and you'll get pleasantly high."

I sucked in the smokey vapors as Alice sang and the hippies twirled and danced. *Am I a pot smoker now*? Blowing it out I instantly thought of the hawk and looked back at the dead tree snag, but it wasn't there. Handing back the pipe, Allison offered, "Let's walk around, take in the sights. Do some people watching."

10:46 am

We headed for the water truck where Louie was doing his thing, watering the masses. The mud had dried some but there was litter on the ground everywhere; cigarette butts, beer and pop can tabs, bits of cellophane, somebody's lost shoe, empty books of matches, pieces of plastic yellow rope, and a muddy sock. As we walked the soft murmur of pacific conversations underscored the occasional whistle or call-out between songs as the scent of western red cedar combined forces with the marijuana in my head, it filled my senses with tingling perceptions of satisfaction.

I had to laugh to myself when we saw people sitting on a sofa enjoying the music, smoking cigarettes and passing weed just like they were at home watching TV. One had an extra-large sombrero on his head; there was a half-eaten watermelon at their soiled feet and an empty cardboard beer container. Up ahead a man in moccasins and denim was leading a burro by a length of thick hemp rope with a young girl on the donkeys back. An American flag for a saddle, with one flying from the end of a stick she held in her hand, a big smile on her face. *Are we living in biblical times*? This movement of fascinating and unbound people had erupted right up out of the soil, taking root, blooming, growing, becoming a life force of human nature that nourished and fed each other's spirit. We were all balanced momentarily in the blissful ether of a tactile event. A point in time that marked time, and history. Sky River held time motionless in a state of perfect grace, the living embodiment of a transcended interval of life, unencumbered by the past in a profound and new contemporary way.

The vendor area had been expanded overnight. There was a new booth where a petite Asian woman and her young daughter were making sandwiches, a stack of premade pizzas in boxes sat behind them. Next to them two new brightly colored stands had been erected with love beads, baubles, scented candles, jewelry and quotation buttons for sale, another was set up for soul-food. Near them, an enormous pile of trash completely covered a string of already filled garbage cans.

"Alright! Let's hear it! Alice Stewart Thomas everyone!" Buddha said to the cheering crowd. "How's everybody doing? Is everybody gettin' high and gettin' by? It's all good! Right? Okay, next up we've got Big Mama Thornton. She's come up from the Bay Area with her blues band to be here today. Let's hear it now for Big Momma Thornton!"

A large black woman with short hair wearing a long white print dress walked out onto the stage smiling broadly and waving to the crowd. She stepped up to the microphone and planted herself in front of it with confidence. Then with a booming voice she cried, "Hello Sky River! Hello Sultan, Washington!" As she did so, the band walked out and pugged in their guitars, the drummer sat down at the kit and the piano man set a beer down next to himself.

"This first one we're gonna do I recorded way back in '52. I was the first singer to do *Hound Dog,* way before that skinny little kid from Memphis did it," she said with a flip of her hand, “and we’s a-gonna play it right now for all you good people here at Sky River! Are you boys ready? Alright, okay, turn it up. Let’s give it to ‘em.”

The band started the intro, her arms began swaying to the rhythm, then her shoulders, then her whole body like she was dancing, but her feet stayed firmly planted in one place. With the power and thunder of the heavens she opened her mouth and tore into the song with sheer abandon, screaming with pain and misery.

Some man was coming around to her house, He was a Hound Dog wagging his tail, Told her that he’s got class, But she’s not so sure about that, Because she ain’t gonna feed him no more.

Her raw howls and grumbles got the crowd to their feet as she commanded the stage and moaned out her lyrics. She was big and bad in her demeanor and delivered her vocals with overwhelming strength in complaint of her freeloading man. It felt like we were in the middle of a storm, or a brawl in a Chicago alley.

“Man, Big Mama is bringing the blues today! She is something.”

"Absolutely. She's the real deal, that's for sure. I wonder how she got those scars on her face?"

"I was wondering that too. She's obviously lived a rough life."

At the songs end Big Mama bowed to the crowd as they screamed for more. People started flooding to the edge of the stage as she beamed with delight. "Okay, okay everyone! You like that? You like it?" Mama said. She walked back to the drums, picked up a brass harmonica and slowly sauntered back to the mic.

"Happy Labor Day, everybody!" she said to cheers. "Well, youse all got the day off but we's a gonna work it real hard for y'all today," she said chuckling. "This next one is, *Everything's Gonna Be Alright*. Hit it boys!"

She ripped the mic out from its stand and cupped it with the harp in both hands as the guitarist picked out a high tone intro, the bass and drums came in and she began to wail on her harmonica so loud that it pierced my ears. Mama makes the harp cry and moan, it's as if it's part of her body as she gyrates and blows the blues while the guitar player responds to her call. They go back and forth and then she renders pure emotion.

Her baby needs to call, She wants him to whisper on the telephone, Says she's given him everything he needs, She wants her lover so bad, Doesn't want him to leave her alone, Everything's Gonna Be Alright.

Big Mama intones a line then blows lonesome on her harp, the guitar man riffs off a quick reply and she wails some more. They go back and forth and build the song into a fire so hot that they nearly combust. Guttural moans of poor outcomes emanate from her, not only from her vocal cords, but from her whole being as she gyrates in pain for her man, her lover.

She asks her man to come on baby, Come on and sit with me, Pleads to come on home baby, You need to take a chance with me, Hurry baby, Everything's Gonna Be Alright.

She slowly steps towards the piano player and calls out to him with her harp, blasting into the cosmos and stops, he replies right back to her, and then the whole bands builds, and climbs, and pushes the song into a howling, screaming, moaning, emotional climax that howls in the torment of heartache and agony of the blues. The music is crying for love and hope in utter human abandonment and loneliness, it's almost too much to bear, my body begins to break and buckle from the sheer force of emotion that flowed outward from Big Mama and her band. They are an unbelievable force of energy and overbearing muscle.

"This is almost too much for me," Allison says. "How about if we go up to our little spot and watch it?"

"Good idea." My stomach was churning and I was about to fall over from the intensity and tilted my head to signal walking, so Allison started out. While Big Mama drenched the crowd with a torrent of passionate blues, we slowly made our way. Glancing back and forth from the ground to watch my step while enjoying the sights to be seen, some cloud cover began to make its way in from the west filtering the sunshine.

11:56 pm

Allison followed a rutty trail that had formed from all the foot travel as we trudged past hundreds of youth troupers and day trippers, many of them new folks that I hadn't noticed in the last two days. One couple had fashioned a gray tarp into a tipi using limbs from the forest for poles, they laid in the opening with their feet hanging out. Another group had strung a number of hammocks between a few trees forming a triangle with a campfire in the middle. An American flag hung between two hemlocks and impromptu huts held up with sticks and limbs provided shelter for hundreds when Big Mama finished her incendiary song.

"Thank you everyone. Now I'm a gonna do a song that I wrote and did years ago, the record company never released it. *Ball and Chain* made Janis Joplin famous last year at Monterey so I let her record it on her great new album. I hope you like my original version of it."

Dominant blues, Watching the rain fall, Why does her man keeps doing her wrong? She sang the song with so much power and emotion it sent cold shivers down my spine. Then she snarled how everything her man was doing made her feel like her whole life was held down by his ball and chain. Mama stomped her feet and howled like a dying woman whose life was lived in vain.

Sure enough, up ahead a couple of bohemians, a man and a woman, had overtaken our little spot. The moss-covered log was now home for a cooler propped up with a pile of rocks. They'd strung rope between trees at the edge of the forest out to wooden poles that they'd whittled from broken limbs and fashioned an ersatz tent with a green canvas tarp for a roof and old visqueen for walls. They sat under it on a small oriental rug and colorful blankets smoking weed. The fellow got up and went to the cooler, bent over it, holding a cup under the drain spout, pouring himself what looked like red wine. He looked up through a head of hanging hair and joyfully said, "Good morning!"

"It is," I replied. He looked to be in his late twenties, wore a white Elizabethan shirt with ruffles and his bellbottom jeans had leather cross-stitching running down the seams. Beads hung from his neck, bracelets of silver and turquoise were wrapped around his wrists, a pair of worn-out caiman leather boots were on his feet. They seemed sophisticated in a shabby chic kind of way and for some unexplained reason he had a presence that evoked a hipster dandy, a libertine Lothario.

"Whatcha got there?"

"It's my own version of spodiodi. Ya' want some? We made it to share!" He opened the cooler so we could look inside. It was a dark liquid, ice, lemons and limes floated in it. "I started with five bottles of port wine, a half-pint of bourbon, and a splash of Bali Hai. It's got everything you'll ever need and then some!" he said with a wink and a nod.

"It's mighty fine. Makes me feel so good all the time!" his woman added. She stood up, blonde hair down to her waist, a white gypsy blouse and a beaded choker around her neck. She gave her man a big sloppy kiss, poured herself a drink then sauntered back to her spot and sat down.

"Oh, gosh, no thank you," Allison said. "Too early."

"No *problemo,*" Lothario answered. "Stop by later, okay?"

"Sure, maybe later. You folks have yourselves a good day."

Allison led us to an open space just down the way and stopped. "The Beats used to drink spodiodi at poetry readings, but not with Bali Hai or fruit. They'd pour a small amount of whiskey into a shot glass then fill it with port. Did you want some?"

"Oh, that's interesting, but no, too early like you said. I've got some water in my canteen if you're thirsty?" I asked, setting down the pack.

"Please."

When I opened up my rucksack for the water Allison saw the notebook. "Can I see what you've written again?"

Without thinking I handed it over and opened the canteen. Allison took a short drink then started reading. *Oh, no! The poem I wrote last night is in there!*

As she worked her way through the pages, turning them over as she perused, I tapped the side of my leg, nervously.

While she read, a brown Chevy station wagon followed by a Ford Econoline pulled right up near the stage. Two women, both long-haired beauties, got out of the Chevy with what looked like overnight bags. Next a dark-haired fellow with four or five cameras hanging from his neck exited the Econoline who was followed by six dudes, three of them carried guitar cases. One guy had a bushy head of black hair and beard, wore a black shirt with vertical-colored stripes, boots over his blue jeans, and carried a beat-up brown guitar case. He stood out from the others. People instantly made way for them; it was as if the dignitaries had arrived. They walked straight to the side entrance to go backstage while one fellow, short with sandy hair, climbed out of the wagon carrying a briefcase and headed for the soundboard controls which had now been fully enclosed in visqueen. Another guy was behind him, carrying a cardboard box, and one who followed everyone backstage with dark hair wearing a denim shirt.

Just then, Allison's eyes sparked. *Uh-oh, I think she just saw the poem.* She started reading out loud.

"A taste of romantic adventure, The Raven she flies in the sun, Music and song moving her, It feels like we've only begun, Hence journey through life and its pages, We turn them together as one, Joyous we sing and we travel, Sky River the magic and mystic, We've won the moment, But still unsung."

"I'm sorry. I write all the time and it felt —"

"You're sorry? It's beautiful. Am I The Raven?" she asked, her expressive blue eyes burning like sapphires.

"Yes, you're the Raven. I didn't mean to be too forward or presumptuous."

Without hesitation she dropped the notebook, grabbed hold of me, pulled me close, then hugged and kissed me, her tongue going deep into my mouth. I did the same, and reached up and held her face in my hands as we embraced surrounded by green forest and freaks. After what seemed like an eternal dream she pulled back and stared deeply into my eyes. "I think you just might be the one," she said. When out of the blue the spodiodi couple erupted in cheers and jubilation.

"Alright! That's the way you do it. Outstanding! Woo-hoo!" Apparently, they'd witnessed our warm embrace.

Blushing, but still hugging her, I said, "I've never felt this way before about anyone. Never, ever. You're so beautiful."

"I feel the same way. Did the first day we met. Just like I said, Fire and Air need each other to survive."

We kept staring into each other eyes and smiling until Buddha interrupted ours and everybody else's train of thought.

"Let's hear it for Big Mama Thornton everyone! Give her a big hand Sky River! Come on! Big Mama! So, remember yesterday when I told you we were working on something for today? Yep, well, it's really happening this time folks," Buddha said as the six hipsters I noticed earlier walked out on the stage. The bearded guy was first, he came out grinning with a black guitar, then a blonde ponytailed fellow who went straight to an amplifier, plugged in his red bass and stood in front of it, adjusting the dials. Two drummers, and a guy with a rumpled-up straw cowboy hat sat at the organ. A young baby-faced fella with a white shirt and brown pants stood talking with the black beard guy, a big red guitar strapped to his shoulder. They all had fresh young faces, full of adventure.

Then Buddha started in, "Quick, turn Phil's mic on. Turn seven on, he's gotta crank up, man. Are you ready? Wait a minute, here we go. Here they are, the people you've been waiting for that you heard about yesterday, the people keepin' it goin' right along. These are the people that started it all . . . The Grateful Dead!" A huge unexpected cheer went up from the astonished crowd. People instantly got up and moved towards the stage, whistling and cheering.

1:37 pm

“Oh, man,” Allison quipped. “Darren loves these guys. He's got both their albums. I have to go; he’ll want to see them.”

“Darren knows about these guys? I think I’ve heard of them.”

“They’re huge down in California. They kinda started the whole hippie scene and now I think they’ve become the scene. Darren would be pissed if he missed them. I have to get back, but you need to stay and work on your article. This will be big.”

“But?”

“No, I insist. I’ll be alright. You might like them,” she said. Allison stepped over and gave me another kiss, then offered, tilting her head at the spodiodi couple, “Hang out with those two, they seem like good people.”

And she was off, headed back down the hill. I watched her the whole way until she disappeared. I glanced over at the two next to me. Lothario with the leather trimmed jeans had his cooler open and was stirring it with a long wooden spoon. He filled his container as the music started and stood up, ecstatic.

"Amazing!" he called out. "Not on the bill. They show up unannounced. I can't believe this. This is huge! Historic! Far-out man! Right here in little old Sultan!"

I listened to the band. Comfortable trippy music, the hirsute bearded guy seemed to be the leader. The three guitarists stood in a tight grouping in front of the drummers, watching each other, playing. Five minutes into the song, the bearded guy started singing and I tried to follow the lyrics.

Spellbinding tale about a Dark Star that's going to strike, But its glow is turning to cinders, A force is bound to unhinge from its center and it's cloudy, Yet we have to run, Through a transient moonbeam of jewels.

Interesting? I'd never heard a voice like his before, full but kind of reedy, he had a way about him on stage that was relaxed. They didn't jump around or move much.

An elfin girl wearing an embroidered white blouse with multiple layers of beads danced in slow motion to the music, her arms moved through the air like a blossoming flower on the wind. She danced for the earth, she danced a vision, she danced a sacrament— she danced a mating call for her favorite band.

"Hey fella!" Lothario next door yelled over the music. "Ready for some wine?" He held up a clear plastic cup.

"Why not." I walked over and he handed me the cup with a grin. I held it under the cooler drain valve, filled it then took a big gulp.

"That's good! Strong and sweet. Thank you."

"You bet."

I stood off to the side of them and listened to the music. Becoming entranced, I lose myself in it. *This isn't regular rock-n-roll, what is it?* The notes speed up and then slow down, they pour out of black beards black guitar like water, clear and clean, very precise. My body starts to tingle, waves of emotion flow through my veins. The music indulges me like nothing ever before and I fold into a transcendent reaction that pulls me into his world. He starts singing again and I become overwhelmed in the song. It floats all around like musical fog and covers me in a hippie contagion of magical mist . . . *I need to get my notebook and pen out.*

A reflector has broken into unformed reactions of madness, While a Dark Star is evolving in a wind of blossoms dying, There's a woman in satin that's returning to an evening of sorrow, Yet we all have to run, Through a transient moonbeam of jewels.

The music doesn't end but it picks up, shifting into a new movement.

There's a well in Saint Stephen's back yard, He goes in and out of his house through a garden in the bright daylight while everyone complains.

They do a few bars of delicate notes then drop into a thick low-end rhythm, the drummers interlocked in a primal pulse that pulls more onlookers towards the stage, they instantly identify with the musicians, clapping to the beat. The band's tribal pace threw us into a vortex of infinite majesty, a swirling musical whirlpool of life.

We wish him well because he's always working, Stephen might get paid and prosper but might not, A woman shows up writing letters of the seasons across the sky.

Then a cameraman stepped onstage taking photos of the band while at the same time from a paint splattered ladder an artisan applied broad graceful strokes of pastel fresco to the stage walls. The music, photography, and artistry thrust the festival into a creative, dynamic feast — a thrilling exotic spectacle of craft and harmonics that had manifested and self-propelled into a place and time that defined a generation. The grand alchemic vision of high art was achieved in a triumphant display of group Zen and was happening before our eyes in real time, transcending the event into a banquet of elevated culture. I'm surrounded with inspiration and my heart is overflowing with joy.

The song changes again and they go into another segment. *They're like a hard rock symphony doing a suite! Black Beard is better than Beethoven —*

His water well is full of spirits, A golden bucket brings the wine, Stephen drinks it all and then sings in the summer sunshine, His hair is so long it's like his home.

"Man, don't you just love The Dead?" Lothario yells over the music, standing next to me, his voice full of spirit, glass empty. He's wavering as he speaks, but keeps his eyes glued to the stage. "Every time I see these guys it's like a religious experience."

"Who's that on lead guitar, the fellow with the beard?"

"That's Jerry Garcia, man, the most far-out player ever," he says with a trickle of sweat running down the side of his face. "I've seen 'em a couple of times at the Eagles. Bob Weir's on rhythm guitar, he kinda supports Jerry and sings. Phil Lesh the bass player, he's like this Stockhausen avant-garde composer, and then the two drummers, Billy Kreutzmann and Mickey Hart. Billy's more of a R&B drummer where Mickey's a marching band guy, and Pigpen on organ. He's total blues. They were Kesey's house band for the Acid Tests."

Acid tests? Pigpen? I don't care if this is anarchy. I love it!

Then it shifts again into a medieval type melody with calliope-like organ that had a lightness to it. I instantly felt like I was in King Aurthur's Court at a Renaissance Faire.

Chilly winds blow green vines, The ground is covered with ivy that shines in the breeze, The children are drinking fresh water from a garden well, Then William Tell arrives with a bow and arrow.

Boom! There they go again. The last one didn't even stop and off we go into a fast rocker and they are cookin'! The two drummers are attacking the song with polyrhythmic intertwining beats that produce a dynamic mixture of tribal enrichment. Garcia starts to challenge them, building, climbing, moving off into space, they slow down, then it builds again, fearless. Jerry shifts into a series of triplets, the organ does a riff just as Garcia unleashes a flurry of ascending notes, the root melody pounded out by the ponytailed Lesh on bass, the drummers kicking behind them when Jerry turns into a primal taskmaster running notes up and down all round us in a swirling, twirling arrangement of time-traveling rock music, a never-ending electric orchestra of all-encompassing sound.

Roaring thunder erupts from Lesh's bass, he's dropping chordal bombs with strokes of intuitive magic that blast over the audience and shake our bones. *I've never heard or even knew of a bass being played like that.* He's creating a whole new form of bass guitar work and not just playing one note at a time; he's reinventing the instrument by playing chords!

The Grateful Dead are creating more than just music; they're building a world of sensory impact. A universe so vast that trying to find one's way back home was useless. They were creating a shelter in real time where you could lay your head, like a road map to a better place, a compass, a path pointing the way to follow to a higher form of life towards the grand creation. Like a magical gift, a creative colossal work of paradisiacal music and wisdom, alive and breathing.

An intertwining story with no meaning, But there's a reason of why it's so, Yet it's not time to return there, With thoughts of gold and silver that shine and sparkle, It's a time to reflect believing.

People streamed to the front of the stage, the space between the band and the audience became seamless. They both were one, all like-minded, all coming together, all in the same hippie garb, living the same credo. It was difficult to distinguish the band from the crowd. The music came first; image was an unknown, unspoken word.

But now is the rest of our lifetimes, It's moving us back to redemption, Tossed on the pile of learning, There's no more time to tell how, We'll discover the reason for what's next and why.

Garcia explodes into a maelstrom of notes, he's a highly charged electrical monster, his fingers fly across the neck of his guitar, it feels like we're going to take off into the stratosphere when for some unexplained reason, I begin to feel fuzzy. I see physical black notes rising out from his amplifier, then a treble clef, more notes, and a bar line floats out, my teeth begin to tingle, my jaw tightens.

Wow! These guys are really good! How do they do that?

An undercurrent of energy shoots through my body, a life-enhancing tingle of spiritual bliss and happiness. I'd never felt more alive and in the moment. More notes pour out of his amp, the drummer's sticks start to glow and flash as the two of them pound away, pushing onward, ascending, going, going, going, until it slows down. Garcia steps to the mic and begins singing.

An intonation that every day we're marking

time, But the sun is blocked, Dissolving, Suddenly its shining the clouds are gone, The leaves begin to grow like children, They're teaching us how we're learning, But everyone was looking, To watch books die.

Off they go again with the wind at their backs, Garcia leading the way, farther, further. He spins a web of notes that rise up from his amp, then orchestra charts of scoring paper float out, filling the atmosphere, all coming together forming a whirling dervish, round and round, above the crowd, they meld into a high-speed chase with Garcia whipping them into a hysteria that changes into color and light, a kaleidoscope of circus magic. Rainbow velvet hues form patterns of light, the notes, bar lines, and charts become intertwined in the air, they turn into brilliant green ivy vines, growing together into a giant beanstalk that climbs, spinning, twisting upward towards the heavens while the crowd dances like jungle animals. Legs kicking, arms flying, couples gyrate like spinning tops, twirling, other people, singles, zigzag and dart between them, more do modern freestyle dance, some run wildly like salmon swimming upstream yet unnoticed. All of them nonjudgmental, pure freedom in its basic form. Expressive movements, all carefree and living wild. Loving life, spurning death, reimagining the world. Laughing, singing, enjoying. Just when I didn't think the music could go any faster, it does, and the other one starts singing an anthem that flew into the sun.

There's a Spanish woman who sings, Her voice is like a rose, It's lovely to see, Like a rainbow but explodes, It spins around then implodes, But it's too hot to touch, So we laugh it off and smile about a cosmic day.

Was he singing to me? Hey, wait a minute, I stepped onto a bus yesterday. Was Allison the Spanish woman? It was as if my whole life flashed before me — a life-changing mark in time, and a life-affirming moment all at once. I'm surrounded by inspiration and my heart starts to race. A landscape of sound and tonal qualities builds into a dreamscape of latitudes and I become overwhelmed with thoughts and emotions. Finishing the rest of the spodiodi, I set the empty cup down, and then gripped my pen with all my might.

We're running through a meadow field, And come upon some magical place, The wind begins to howl, It brought a bus lost from space, The door it opened and we got on, There was a cowboy behind the wheel, Then everyone left behind the human race.

Whoa, everything's out of whack — what's happening to me?

2:47 pm

I looked over at Lothario guy, him and his woman look out of focus, but dancing, twirling to the music. Garcia's still playing away, the music is pounding. The crowd is going nuts, when, what on earth — the scene changes — everybody turns into Gumbys, just like the cartoon. I look at my hands, they're Gumby hands. My wino buddies next to me, Gumby, the band, Gumby, and the burro is Pokey! Wow! . . . Wait a second! I'm in cartoon land and it's fantastic. Even Betty's house was a colorful clay pastiche, vibrant. Everybody's moving in a stop-motion way, skinny arms and flat wide legs and bodies, rubbery, bending with jerky movements, everyone's made out of clay. I look at my legs, they're flat and wide and really green!

When everything changes again — now I'm a pirate Gumby. I've got on a black tricorne hat and the pen in my hand grows into a gleaming cutlass. The crowd below turns into an ocean of swashbuckling humanity in silk bandanas, sailcloth pants, velvet vests with jeweled trim, peg legs, and there's crashing waves of seawater behind me. Off I run with my jewel encrusted sword, ready to do battle with privateers and find buried treasure. *I must take my ship, The Walrus, and slay anyone that gets in my way!* I sprint through a forest of green Gumby trees then come across a salty lagoon filled with naked pirate swimmers, beautiful unclad Gumby girls, all cavorting with fellow scalawags, splashing, laughing, diving for gold doubloons and Spanish pieces of eight. Ferns grow into palm trees with silver fronds that ring the water, while more nymphs and cherubs arrive to frolic along the sandy shore in wanton abandon. A flirtatious female of nubile delight eyes me with a come-hither look, oozing of earthy lust. My internal fun meter ticked up to eleven and my mind lit up like a pinball machine.

"Avast, me hearties! For I am Cap'n Flint McCalister, here to maraud and pillage with all yee buccaneers!" I yell, holding my cutlass out in front of me. "I shall set sail on my ship, The Walrus, and find more Spanish gold than all of you will ever see!"

In a fit of laughter and hilarity the crew in the lagoon only laughs at my proposal. In defiance, I drop my backpack, rip off all my clothes, the deputy's business card flying out of a shirt pocket, and then dive into the lagoon in a stunning display of daring do and high-seas action. They all laugh and enjoy the circus side-show that has just shown up until the sharp tip of my sabre breaks the water's surface in a gallant display of gallantry and valor, the jewels on its hilt sparkling.

"Are you ready to spoil and plunder for booty and gold! Or are you just a bunch of worthless landlubbers! You! Sprite wench! Come with me and we shall sail the seas in search of treasure and doubloons!"

Death Don't Have No Mercy, Death Don't Have No Mercy? It's gonna come to my home? My wife and kids will be gone? Death will leave me lost and crying? Now?

"Hey man!" a surly looking Gumby with wet stringy hair hollered, his shaggy virility agape, reminiscent of Pan. "Quit pointing at my old lady! Fuckin' stop it!"

"Ah, but the nubile little harlot beckons me to take her away on The Walrus! I can see it in her eyes. She is my Aphrodite!" — then angry Gumby guy shape-shifts into a mutant version of Pan, the stink of the rut instantly fowls the air and Pan was in it. *Holy Crap! Pan! The God of the wild!* Horns grow from his head, goat legs of clay with cloven hooves and a goat tail appears. He's covered in greasy matted hair and his voice is now a deep dark echo.

"Didn't you hear what — I fucking said . . . man! Or are you, out of your mind? Because I will beat the ever-lovin' shit . . . out of you if you don't stop staring at my woman — my old lady! Stop It, NOW!"

Death Don't Have No Mercy. How long will it stay? It's still coming to my place? In my bedroom? Death? Today? And my siblings are all gone? Death Don't Have No Mercy.

But then Pan's woman looks at me with terror in her eyes — *What? — She's Allison!! And with him!* — Shock and horror bolt through my system, my blood boils into a rage of loathing and I point my cutlass at him and scream.

"You have absconded with my Allison and for that you shall pay the ultimate price! I know you want to live and never feel the tip of my sword! Fear not, my Allison," I exclaim, slashing the cutlass through the ether. "I will save you and take you back to be at my side!"

Death Don't Have No Mercy. Everywhere?! My people are gone? Death is coming to my home! Now? Today?

"That's it! You fucking bastard! Get out of the water!"

"So it's a duel then! But I must warn you, I am a master of the sword and my blade will strike you down!"

Instantly the brooding naked Pan hulk gallops at full speed with his head down, ready to ram into the lagoon after Captain McCalister. Pan charges into the pond at the same time that Cap'n Flint charges at him. They tussle in the turbulent water but Pan quickly gains the upper hand and grabs him by the neck with a giant hairy fist, then stands up dragging the pirate onto the bank.

"Unhand me you, uncouth swine of Pan. You louse! Release me or I will sic my faithful crew upon you!"

"No Eddy! Don't!" Pans real girlfriend screams, running to get her towel and cover herself. The other women do the same.

"I'll teach you to talk to my old lady like that you little punk!" Hirsute Pan yanks him across the beach and pandemonium ensues. Screams and hollers fly from every woman's throat as Pan throws the pirate to the ground. Looming over his victim, he raises an ugly fist and was about to strike when —

"HE'S A NARC! The guy's a sheriff! Look! I found his card on the ground! The little fucker's a god damn Narc!"

The scene changes — now Pan is Eddy again, he snaps his head around to see the other man waving a white card. "So, you're a Narc and a mother fucking mouthy little runt who tried to steal my woman! You're not long for this world. Lights out time!"

Death Don't Have No Mercy, It's going to leave me alone and crying but not stay long? No! It's not coming to my place today, Or any other day! No Death!

"Go fuck yourself you Narco Cop Sheriff weirdo!" Eddy raised his clenched fist again when a new voice screamed.

"STOP IT! He's not a Narc!" The flash of a body flies sideways>>>>through the air, tackling Eddy before he could strike.

Holy Jesus! What just happened! They roll across the ground and my cartoon life ends. A woman quickly jumps up, daggers in her eyes, the anger in her voice sharp and pointed. *What*?!? – It's the real Allison!!

"THAT'S ENOUGH!" she screamed. "He's stoned on acid or something . . . He's obviously hallucinating! And he's not a Narc," she barked, running over to the fellow with the sheriff's card and ripping it from his hands.

"He's a reporter and saw a crime this morning at the Sultan motel. The Sherrif wanted a statement."

Heads turn back and forth as a momentary hush fell over the scene.

"Well, if he's not a Narc, then he's a lousy snitch!"

"Cliff isn't a snitch. And he's not going to call the Sheriff," she hollered, ripping the card in pieces then tossing them on the ground.

"There! Happy now?"

"Well okay," Eddy lamented. "But if he's none of those things and if his name is Cliff, then who in the hell is Flint McCalister? Riddle me that — little lady?"

Eyes glance back and forth between all the players, including me, who was no longer a pirate, but my body still buzzed with electricity. I scratched my head, stood up and then looked down at myself. *Why am I naked!?!* Darren began gathering up my clothes and rucksack then carried them over to me, saying, "You, okay? Teresa didn't want to come back for the Dead. Good thing Allison did."

A current of energy hummed through my system as I quickly got dressed, Allison walked over to us. I was giggling and babbling at the same time, "I'm sorry — I'm sorry. I don't . . . know what happened." Then I looked at her, she smiled a sweet smile. I gave her a big hug and whispered in her ear, “I’m sorry. Thank you, forever.”

Allison pulled away, looked deep into my eyes then quietly said, “I’ll do anything for you, and I just proved it.”

“So, did you drink anything?” Darren asked, breaking our moment. “Or take something? It was probably LSD or it could have been that other stuff I’ve heard of, DMT I think they call it.”

I tried to search my mind, but my body was overcome with shimmering sparks of magnetism, and buzzing with inner body sensations. I was feeling both bullet proof and fragile at the same time. Then the light green tips on the fir tree branches began to glow and flicker. “I think, well . . . does anybody else see that? The tips of the tree limbs are really bright, um, so, I’m trying to think, I believe I had a glass of wine that guy had . . . you know, the Lothario guy with the cooler.”

“Lothario? Who’s that? What? Oh, right?” Allison said, glancing at the tree branches and shaking her head. “We just talked with them, they said you ran off up here.”

In the meantime, all the skinny dippers had lost their lust for life and gotten dressed while the air, the trees, the ground, and the music crackled like eggs in hot butter. It felt like I was surrounded by multiple charged fields of energy.

Walking away Allison joked, “I guess we just can’t take you anywhere.” But then she snickered and Darren laughed.

“I’m sorry. It’s,” I croaked, stumbling a little, “I was . . . the guy asked if I’d like some wine, so I did, sure. Then the Grateful Dead started traveling, um, no, playing. I liked the music, and pretty soon I saw notes, like real physical notes — floating out of Garcia’s amplifier and then I turned into Gumby, like the cartoon.”

“You turned into . . . *Gumby*!” Allison blurted, reacting with shock but in a kind of happy way because I was alright.

“Yep, just like on Saturday morning, but everyone was Gumby too. The crowd, the band, up at the pond. Even the cute little burro — it turned into Pokey!"

"Jesus, Cliff," Darren said. "That must have been scary. Sounds like you had an orchestra of psychedelics playing in your head."

"It was. I did. But it didn't scare me at all. I just kinda went along for the ride and watched everything go into looney tunes." After a pause, I said, as the muddy trail under my feet began to ooze molten silver and gold, "Thank you for showing up just in time and saving me from probably a pretty good ass kicking . . . or worse."

"Yeah, you did a really good job of pissin' that guy off. What on earth did you say up there to make him so mad?"

"I'm not sure," I replied, watching the ooze turn turquoise, then back to silver and gold, "because I turned into a pirate."

"*What*?!?"

"I know it sounds odd, but I had a Gumby sword and a beautiful pirate ship — does anyone else see the colors? The silver and gold mud that's under our feet?"

Allison turned around and gawked at me just as the stage came into view. I stopped walking and became consumed in whole. The guitarists were shoving their instruments up against amplifiers, Pigpen was on his feet pushing his organ, slamming it, and the drummers were striking and crashing cymbals like lightning, when my shoulders relaxed. I closed my eyes, let my arms hang at my side with open palms, and then lost myself to the soul awakening volcanic sounds of *Feedback*.

In a flash of super-sonic overdrive I'm transported to an unknown place — a wide ranging network of images and questions move through my cortex — where does consciousness exist — what is the nature of my existence — a vehicle of cataclysmic tones carries me on a soundwave defying gravity — in a real-time retina scan I see visions of creation and revelations of life — a river of ecstasy — fever dreams of molecular energy — then destruction — pivotal axis rotation unturns — the moon crashes into the earth — afterburners of a starship scream into the fundamental laws of physics — yin and yang noises of black and white — pink and blue — atomic mushroom catastrophe looms — red rockets glare opposed to injustice — Stockhausen vibrations pierce the atmosphere — life death birth childhood — my father's open arms — a crying newborn marks time — sirens wail — absolute celestial freedom — archetypal church bells throng — seeds germinate rapidly — a slammed door unlocks — keys tossed to the rain — a soft summer wind carries butterflies home to safety — interstellar craft descends to a reconstructed culture — rainbows appear — I receive new magical insight and accelerated learning — a soft hand touches my palm — I open my eyes to color and tenderness.

It's Allison, a smile of true understanding on her face. "You're still tripping, aren't you?" she says, taking me by the hand and leading me, dazed, down the trail.

"Let's hear it for the Grateful Dead!" Buddha shouted. "They're probably pretty tired. They just played a lot down south, then they came up here for us. Bob, if I was you, I'd be asleep right now. The Grateful Dead!"

3:18 pm

At the party site, Darren opened the cooler. It was empty, save for a few pieces of fruit and some melting ice cubes. Lothario and his woman had absconded into their visqueen makeshift tent. Lusty moans and groans came from behind the opaque screen. She was on top of him in a heated act of lovemaking, grinding, bouncing, both of them naked, besotted with mind altering chemicals.

"I'm thinkin' we should leave them alone," Darren offered.

A cleansing relief of satisfaction moved through my body and I began to come back to reality. As we walked through the festivities, I opened the backpack, my notebook and everything else was inside. *Good. I'm glad that didn't disappear!* The crowd was still basking in spiritual balm from the Dead's appearance; enlightened faces and blissful smiles were everywhere. The fellow I'd seen earlier with the briefcase at the soundboard went by us grinning with the spacy look of serenity, his wire-rimmed glasses down on his nose, hair frazzled. His myopic look and watery eyeballs told me he'd either gotten shocked by high-voltage electrical current or had gone through a similar encounter to mine. He was murmuring softly to himself and stutter stepping along, as if one foot was afflicted with the hiccups and the other had the giggles.

"I think that was Owsley, maybe," Darren remarked.

"Who?"

"Owsley Stanley. They call him the acid king; he makes LSD and is the Dead's soundman. He bankrolled them for their first couple of years, bought equipment, paid their rent. The guy's a genius."

"How do you know all that stuff?" I asked.

"Oh, I don't know, well, I guess I do. I'm a big follower of Ken Kesey, the writer. He used to do Acid Tests with his group of followers called the Merry Pranksters."

"I saw his book in your bus, *Sometimes a Great Notion.*"

"Great book, great writer. The Dead were the house band for his Acid Tests. He wrote another book, *One Flew Over the Cuckoo's Nest.* Have you heard of it?"

"I have."

Savoring a moment of peaceful tranquility, I gazed out at all the beautiful people as we ambled along when on the other side of the crowd, I saw two long-haired fellows pulling a large piece of what looked like a green dirty tarp. Focusing in I noticed bits of yellow on it and suddenly realized. *That's the carpet! The motel thieves!* There was a group of fun-seekers following them, it looked like they were moving to a new spot. I laughed out loud, pointing and saying, "Haha! Hey! It's carpet guys!" Darren and Allison stopped and looked at me. "Way over there," I said, gesturing.

"Oh, my gawd, that's funny," she said peering in their direction. "Good thing I ripped up that sheriffs card."

“What? Who is it?” Darren asked.

“We’ll tell you all about it later,” Allison replied, grinning.

“Okay everybody, how we doin’ out there?” Buddha said, interrupting our conversation. “We’ve got It’s a Beautiful Day coming up in just a few minutes, so hang tight, don’t go anywhere!”

“Oh, man, nice!” Darren exclaimed. “Teresa wants to see them.”

“We need to go and get her. Cliff and I will watch the kids.”

“Really? Because that’d be great. She’d love that.”

Down at the county road we didn’t have to wait long for the shuttle bus to take us to the campground. We watched as smiling people and local kids got off then we boarded. Allison and I sat next to each other while Darren sat behind the driver and opened his window.

“So, what really happened to you?” Allison asked quietly.

"Well, I think what really happened was that my life transformed right in front of me. Whatever it was that I took opened my mind, it was like self-discovery. I got reprogrammed. And I still have this wonderful warm buzz inside of me."

"Yes, but you were completely naked up at the pond."

"Oh, yeah, that. I don't know how it happened. Like I said, I went all Gumby and it just, well, I guess it just felt natural to strip down and get buck naked and dive in. So, I guess it was a normal reaction. Everybody was skinny dipping and my mind was blown."

"But you were on the ground, and he was naked too. He was about to hit you so you must have said something."

I searched my mind, then said, "I'm not completely sure, but I think I hallucinated that he had stolen you, or captured you, and that he was going to take you away on his pirate ship. So, I challenged him to a duel."

"You what?! I what?!"

"I know it sounds crazy but that guy had turned into Pan and I was totally lost in being a pirate, like a real pirate and my pen turned into this beautiful sword. But he had stolen you from me and I was going to fight him to get you back."

Allison rolled her eyes at me and said, "He'd stolen me? And you were going to fight him with your invisible pen sword? That is *so* cute. You were going to duel it out over me — sounds like old fashioned chivalry. But wait a second. So, was I naked, too?"

"Mmm, yes, I think you were, but Gumby naked."

"Okay, so, you think you saw me *Gumby* naked and I know for sure that I saw you *real* naked. Well," she sighed, "I believe you." Allison smiled her sweet smile of serenity and continued, "I sure liked seeing you naked. You've got a cute little butt." Then she whispered, "Maybe I'll show you my tattoo later. Unless you saw it, already?"

"Oh, gosh. I don't think I remember any tattoo."

As we turned into the campground it looked empty, save for Teresa sitting outside at the tables with Bodhi and Lydia who were playing on their blanket.

“Here we are folks,” said the driver over his shoulder.

“Can you wait just a minute. My wife and I want to go back?”

“Sure, no problem. But I’ll have to drop you off at the Ben Howard because I have to turn left and go the long way back. It’s only open one way today, the wrong way.”

“That’s still a lot closer. Thanks, I’ll be right back.”

With a huge smile Teresa jumped up at the sight of us walking towards her. Darren picked up his daughter and held her on his hip for a moment and patted his son on his head. “How are you kids doing? Everything okay? It’s a Beautiful Day is going to play next.”

“I heard, and all’s good here at the fort, so,” Teresa said, standing up.

"Allison and Cliff are going to watch the kids and the bus driver's going to wait for us. Let's hurry."

"Fantastic!" Teresa said with delight. "The kids just ate and you know what to do," she said, looking at Allison. "Just lemme get my old shoes on and I'll be ready."

She bolted onto their bus, returned in a flash and they were off, running with glee to the shuttle and head back. Just as she was about to follow Darren aboard, Teresa turned and shouted, "Have fun you two, see you in a while and don't do anything I wouldn't do!"

Allison grinned at her sister then waved. She picked up Lydia and said to her, "I don't think Cliff has seen the tipi yet. How about if we take him to the magic tipi? Come on Bodhi, you too, bring Cliff and we'll see what's in the tipi today. Maybe there'll be a pirate!"

Laughing to myself when she said it, I picked up Bodhi. His little legs were kicking as I carried him through the low opening and then set him gently down inside.

4:20 pm

Persian rugs covered the floor, overstuffed cushions with tapestry coverings lay about, a couple of sleeping bags and an antique end table with a brass Buddha incense burner. A few small seashells were on it completing the ambiance. The evening sunset cast its light against a sky of soft clouds that could be seen through the upper opening, the support poles cleanly trimmed and shellacked. A tube of Lincoln logs was on the rugging. Bodhi ran straight for them and dumped them out.

"Good," Allison said to her nephew. "You and your sister can build a log cabin. How about some sandalwood?" She stepped over to the table and got out some incense, lit it with her ever-handy matches while I gathered up some pillows for us then laid down with my head on a cushion. Allison dropped down beside me and exhaled, "*That,* was quite a day."

"Okay everyone, I'm Cyrus Noe, the general manager of the festival. The Sultan townsfolk and law enforcement were most helpful this weekend. I've changed roles at the time to end what in its final hours was purely delightful. I took over as emcee and chose It's a Beautiful Day to play the final set and end the show. This indeed was, a beautiful day!"

The drummer started a beat; the organ came in and the strings of a violin began to pick out a melody. The band slowly builds the song into a trippy, light series of lovely notes. My body tingles at the incantation. It makes me feel alive and present, happy. Then two voices, a man and a woman begin to sing in perfect harmony, his is deep and clear, hers floating above. It sounds like classical music set to a modern rock beat.

A White Bird is trapped in a cage, Every day and it's raining, The White Bird is all by herself, The wind is blowing trees that bend, Under dark black skies, In her gilded cage, Alone, Yet the White Bird shall fly for you and I.

They sing like angels on high. I'm overwhelmed with where the music goes. Gypsy violin transports us into celestial ether. I glance over at Allison, she's lying on her side, looking at me with coquettish eyes. Time stops; we travel with melodic notes and chants to newborn revealing's.

“I do believe that I’ve fallen into the full embrace of things. You, your family, everything this weekend has been warm, inviting, and fulfilling. When I first got to Sultan, I wasn’t really feeling very good about this assignment and all. I didn’t know anything about this kind of life or the people who lived it. Here I was a guy from Spokane, unversed in the ways of the hippie idiom, a rookie I guess and not really happy in life. I mean, I was, kinda. My job’s okay and all but, um, I really wasn’t content. I think my soul was starved and lacking nourishment. But then on the first day of the festival you sat down next to me, it was unbelievable. With all the thousands of people, you picked me, and I am so incredibly overjoyed that you did.”

“Yes, I remember,” Allison began, “when I first saw you sitting there writing, I was instantly attracted to you and thought, ‘here’s this guy in the middle of a rock show composing his thoughts, a guy who can think things through.’ To me, you looked studious and focused and I just knew you were on a good path. Doing something true in the middle of thousands of searchers and screamers. But still like all of us here trying to figure it out, while at the same time making your statement, but in writing. It was clear to me that you were chasing your dream, chasing lightning. It was like a satori, or an epiphany for me. You were flying above everyone else. I was immediately impressed. Plus, you looked so cute in your tennis shoes and preppie shirt collar sticking out above your gray sweatshirt. But please, tell me more about you, Mister Pirate."

White Bird has landed on moonlit trees, With it's turning leaves, In autumn, And the White Bird still is alone in a cage, Turning gray, But the White Bird shall fly, But she might die.

"Oh, gosh. So, after today, well, I've been thinking a lot about everything. This whole weekend, I mean, it really has been an adventure and it's opened me to so many new things. This music festival has become a dividing line, my incomplete life before, but now with you, Sky River, Jerry Garcia and the Grateful Dead after. And I've got to say that band is something else. The way they created their music, and it was more than music, it was like they built this vast world that you could get lost in. It was a place that was within the space and time of Sky River and we were all there but someplace else all at once, everyone, everything. The music was all-encompassing and far beyond our solar system, in another galaxy. It held everything, the present, the past, the morning sun, the clouds, lofty peaks, it was a sunrise and a sunset at the same time. I'd never experienced anything like it and then during their feedback segment when Garcia was using his guitar like a rocket ship, they all were, and my life flashed before me. I had all these visions of life and death and so many other revelations."

"Oh yeah, I noticed, and knew you were going through some changes."

"I was, but I have to tell you, on the first day when I rode out here on the shuttle bus and we were riding across the bridge, seeing the clear mountain river water spilling through the valley and the Cascade peaks in the distance, it affected me. This jolt of inner voltage zinged through my body. I'd never gotten that feeling before. And now, after meeting you and feeling the way I do, I understand that the bridge was more than just a span to get across to the other side. It was a bridge to you and a new life. A bridge to a new and better life."

I glanced over to Allison again, she was looking at me intently, deeply, her expressive eyes digging into me.

"As you've probably figured out, I've been a literary obsessive since, well, since forever. When I was little, I'd get lost for days on end reading the books my father got for me. I absorbed all those children's classics like, *Jack and the Beanstalk*, but then I moved on to, *Swiss Family Robinson*, *Robinson Crusoe*, and, *Treasure Island*. I loved *Treasure Island* when I was a kid with Black Dog and Billy Bones. Once I got older, I read *Grapes of Rath*, *Moby Dick* and *East of Eden*, love them, too. The connection of how the prose is transferred to the brain and how the vision that the words create comes to life in the mind's eye has always captivated me. All those books gave me an escape and made me feel good. But not as good as I feel now. Because with everything that's happened this weekend, I've been able to look inside myself. I've discovered how I want to live my life, and what I want to learn, how I want to feel, and act, who I want to be and who I want to spend my life with. It's as if I've gotten a sudden stroke of enlightenment, a bolt of complete understanding."

The music soars, the two voices meld in perfect harmony and it carries us along. The song builds into a climbing rhapsody and the skin on my arms tingles.

Each season comes, Each season goes, The sun shines cold, The land grows old, But the White Bird's wings have flown, White Bird it flies ~~~

"There was a mystique in those books that pulled me into their world, and I loved that. The same kind of mystique that has brought me to you. And maybe I hope, you to me. I feel like my life has been redefined."

I rolled over on my side and put my hand on her hip, she did the same. I gazed into her eyes. She was the most intoxicating woman I'd ever known. And right then, in that exact moment, I knew Allison was the only woman I ever wanted to know or be with. I'd fallen deeply, madly in love with her. There was no turning back. I wanted to be stuck in her gilded cage but never see her fly away, or she would die. We would die.

"I'm in love with you, Allison Fisher. You are the most beautiful creature I've ever known and I want to stay with you forever." She instantly pinched my butt and smiled.

"I already told you I'd do anything for you, remember?"

"Yes."

"Some people say that life itself is reality," she continued, her voice warm and comforting, "others say it's a mystery. However, I like to think of life as a kind of fairytale come true that I'm living minute by minute. But after today, it's occurred to me that when you were deep in the throes of whatever it was that guy dosed you with, you had transferred yourself into a fairytale like state and returned to seeing life through child-like eyes. And that's just the way I want to live. Alive and bright. I want to live a vivid life that glows and radiates, outward and forward. Every single day, like a glowing light.

But not like a beam of light that's concentrated on one spot. I want to glow in every direction, like the sun. I want to glow on you, on us. I want you to know that," she said in earnest. "But for now, all I want to know is, who is, Flint McCalister?"

Blushing I said, "Oh that, um, gosh. So, my dad loved *Treasure Island* when he was a kid and so did I, obviously. But when I was born, he gave me the name, Flint Clifford McCalister. For Captain Flint, of the Walrus, in *Treasure Island*. It's my legal name. I always thought it was silly, so I never used it. I've always just called myself Cliff. I think today, I was reborn."

Allison immediately rolled over on her back and hollered, "Oh, my gawd! I love it! You're Flint McCalister! *Flint McCalister!* I can see it now; it all makes sense. Your writing, your open nature, your willingness to change and grow. The way you've stretched and opened your consciousness this weekend. I've seen you do all these things in the last few days and now I can see it. You need to quit that stupid newspaper job, the one you called antiquated, and start writing novels. Forget *journalism!* You should come and live with me in Oregon, with Darren and Teresa and the kids. At least come and visit me, us. They've got a big old house, plenty of room, or we'll get our own place. I'll start substituting soon, you can get a job at the Journal if you want, they've been in business for a hundred years. But really, you should write literature . . . Oh!" She rolled back over on her side and gazed at me, lovingly.

Then her eyes sparked, beaming of bright sapphire and discovery. She quickly got up on her knees, saying, "Ooh! Ooh!" and straddled me, pinning me in place, then grinned an alluring roguish grin. "You should write about this! The Sky River Rock Festival! And us! It can be your first novel! Now I know what the future holds, it's all completely and perfectly clear! It's in the stars! It's absolute and total destiny!"

Allison bestowed a smile of sweet serenity, magic, and ultimate bliss upon me. She dropped down on top of me and we kissed, our tongues probing deep into each other's mouth, for what seemed like an eternity — pulling away, her expressive blue eyes shined with inspiration and intimacy. She gushed, "We are defined by what, and who we love, and I love you, Flint McCalister. And I will be devoted to you and take care of you, and us, for the rest of our days."

"I too, will be devoted to you, Allison Fisher, and love you endlessly," I promised, pulling her back down to me, holding her close, forever.

White Bird >>> we shall fly ~~~ or we may die >>> White Bird >>> we shall fly ~~~ or we may die ~~~ White Bird >>> we shall fly ~~~~~

Acknowledgements

I'd like to give an appreciative heartfelt thanks to everyone who helped bring this story to a reality. I couldn't have done it without your help! I owe a depth of gratitude to my editor and spiritual advisor Bill White for all of his efforts. Thank you, Bill! I want to thank Joy Tachell of the Sultan Historical Society, along with C. H. Rowe, Tom Sofie and Michael Smith for all of their help. Thank you, Greg Garton of the Sky River Rock Festival '68 Reunion for your insight.

A huge thank you goes out to my creative team; Steve Breeden, Susie Uhl, and Susan Harrell. I would also like to thank Paul Hansen of the Musicians' Association of Seattle for his assistance in my research.

I would be remiss if I did not credit my son Skyler for his guidance and inspiration. Thank you, Skyler, for all your help over the years! I'd also like to thank the following for their contributions: Steve Noe, Tore Ofteness, Gale Fiege, Mike Oshie, David Gans, Kathy Kane, and Karen Ruth Foster Erickson.

For the last 55 years I've had the rewarding life experience of dining on the musical cuisine of Grateful Dead. Thank you for feeding my soul! I want to express my great love and respect for them and all the musicians and artists of the 1960s. I'd like to give thanks to you for your contributions to our times and especially the enrichment of my life. No other decade has produced more significant music to our culture and brought freedom and courage to the minds and ears of so many. The music that grew and flowered in San Francisco in the '60s grabbed me in a profound way, it turned me into the searcher that I still am today. I would also like to pay tribute to John Chambless, Cyrus Noe, Paul Dorpat, those on the Helix staff, Betty Nelson, and all the rest who helped bring about Sky River. Thank you for putting on a defining, seminal event!

In closing, I'd like to clarify my use of paraphrasing lyrics. I made many attempts to communicate through letters, emails, and phone calls, and applied to purchase the lyric rights from Sony Music and Universal Music. But I was unable to secure those rights. However, I felt it was important to reference and honor the performers and their legacy in the narrative, so I chose to paraphrase.

About the Author

Brown Award and Malstrom Award winning author JD Howard was born in West Seattle and raised in Everett, Washington. He is the proud father of two wonderful children and currently lives in the foothills of Snohomish County near Sultan. His other works include: Both Sides of The Wish (2013) Sawdust Empire (2016) The Pride of Monte Cristo (2019) Paper Highway (2020) and French Peter — Journey to Hat Island (2021).

www.ingramcontent.com/pod-product-compliance
Lightning Source LLC
Chambersburg PA
CBHW030540190726
48283CB00006B/1955
* 9 7 8 1 7 3 3 6 0 4 3 5 2 *